LINGER

Edward Fallon

#2

Trail
of the
Beast

BRAUN HAUS MEDIA, LLC

*The publisher wishes to acknowledge
and thank J.D. Rhoades
for his contribution to this work*

Sign up for the
Braun Haus Media, LLC Newsletter
and get a free ebook.

Yes, that's right.
A free full-length supernatural thriller
from our growing library of books.

See BraunHausMedia.com for details

Other books in the *Linger* series available for purchase now

LINGER 2

Trail of the Beast

PART ONE

"If you do not change direction, you may end up where you are heading."

~*Lao Tzu*

1

THE WOMAN SAT IN THE DARK in the gravel parking lot, staring at the red door. She wondered if she might be losing her mind.

She'd packed up, left her life and career as a major crimes detective behind, and driven halfway across the country to this small motel off a forgotten side road in Missouri—because of a voice in her head.

Had she heard a story like that from anyone else, the first thing she would have thought was *nutcase.*

But she knew that voice was real. She knew it belonged to the strange, sightless boy behind that red door. It was a voice she'd first heard at a crime scene halfway across the country, in the living room of a murdered family.

It was a voice that could not possibly exist, and yet it did.

As she sat there, watching, she heard the voice again.

Hello, Kate. Come on in and join us. We saved you some pizza.

The woman shook her head.

Guess there was no backing out now.

She got out of the car and walked toward the red door.

2

"WHAT THE HELL IS HE doing?" Kate Messenger said out loud, leaning forward and squinting through the windshield of her SUV as if the extra few inches could bring the car ahead into clearer focus.

The car slowed, then slowed again. As Kate watched, it veered slowly toward the shoulder of the narrow ribbon of two-lane blacktop they'd been following for hours through the sun-blasted landscape of rural Alabama.

"Damn it," Kate muttered. "I knew that thing was trouble."

The lead car was a relic, a decaying 1964 Rambler Cross Country station wagon that Kate thought should have been junked years ago. Thought, but did not say. At least not more than once. The man driving the Rambler, a man named Noah Weston, had been on this quest longer than Kate, and he'd let her know from the beginning that her opinion of the car—or anything else, for that matter—was not welcome.

I shouldn't have come, she thought for the hundredth time.

Why am I even here?

The answer came in the form of a familiar voice in

her head.

We've got a problem.

In her mind's eye, she could see the source of that voice: the mute boy with the blind white stare who sat in the back seat and to the right of the Rambler's driver.

Christopher.

The boy whose voice had brought her here, to this place, on the trail of a killer.

Kate pulled her vehicle to a stop behind the Rambler. She got out, gasping a little with the shock of stepping into the soggy heat of an Alabama summer from the coolness of the air-conditioned SUV. In moments, she had begun to sweat, the moisture clinging to her skin and clothing, trapped by the saturated air.

Weston was getting out of the car as well. He didn't acknowledge Kate's approach as he walked to the front of the vehicle where the hood had been popped. The old metal creaked a bit as he raised the hood and peered inside.

"What's wrong?" Kate said as she walked up.

"Overheating," he told her. "I turned the AC off to try and cool her down."

She caught a whiff of him. He was drenched in sweat as well. Then she smelled something else: the sharp tang of overheated metal.

"Don't," she said as Weston reached for the radiator cap.

He glared at her, then lightly tapped the top of the cap with two fingers. He drew in his breath with a hiss as he quickly pulled the fingers back.

"Let her cool off," he muttered, half to himself. "Then we can limp her into the next town. Find a repair shop."

"It'll be October before that engine cools. We need to get a tow truck. Or just leave it—"

"We're not leaving my car," Weston snapped, and was about to continue when his gaze shifted past her shoulder. "Hey!"

Kate looked. Christopher had the passenger side door open and was getting out of the car.

"Hey, Chris. Where are you going?" she asked.

They'd been traveling for the last hour through an expanse of flat, fertile land, the fields stretching out on either side bursting with some of the thickest, greenest crops she'd ever seen. She'd recognized some of them, like the corn and cotton, but others were a mystery to her.

In the place where they'd come to rest, however, there was a stand of trees, set back thirty yards or so from the road across a ragged strip of grass. The dark cool shade beckoned to her.

Christopher obviously felt the call, too; he was heading for the grove, not slowing down. She wondered how he knew about the shade. There was no way he could see it, after all. But then, Christopher sometimes seemed to just know things.

Sometimes, it was hard to remember he was blind.

She followed.

Stepping into the grove was like stepping into another world. It felt at least twenty degrees cooler, and Kate almost groaned out loud with relief. The sunlight lanced down through the breaks in the leaves like spotlights, illuminating the forest floor.

Christopher was standing in a small clearing about twenty feet in. He was caught in one of the beams, looking into the light with his sightless eyes. He turned to Kate and smiled.

This is one of the thin places, he said, and she could feel the awe and the joy behind the words.

"The... the what?" she stammered.

He didn't answer, but turned back to the light.

She turned to Weston who was just joining them. "What does he mean?"

Weston shrugged. "Don't know, but it seems to make him happy." He took a deep breath. "Can you feel it?"

"I can feel it's a little cooler in the shade," she said. "That's enough for me." She saw Christopher moving deeper into the woods and called out. "Hey!"

He was almost running now, and Kate was afraid he'd trip on a root and hurt himself.

Can you hear her? Can you hear the singing?

Kate jogged after him. As she caught up to him, she saw that he was following the nearly overgrown vestiges of a path through the woods.

"Hey, kiddo," she said, panting from the heat. "Come on, we're getting too far from—"

Just a little farther.

As he spoke, they came out of the trees.

Kate drew up short. "Wow."

The ground dropped off sharply to a narrow strip of sand, which served as a kind of beach to a broad expanse of dark water. Willows lined the bank, drooping low over the fast moving river. Some of their roots protruded from the dirt, showing where high water had carved at the soil in years past. A few feet away was a strange formation of flat, gray-brown rocks that marched like uneven steps from the land into the river.

"It's beautiful," Kate said.

Christopher's voice filled her head again.

Can you hear her?

Kate strained her ears, but all she could hear was the slight breeze rustling the willows and the soft trickle of the water over the flat stones.

This is where she comes to sing, he said.

Then Kate felt the shock of his realization.

This is where he killed her.

•

When Weston caught up to them he said to Chris, "Who are you talking about? Was it *him*?"

Kate didn't need to ask who he meant.

No, Christopher said. *Not him. Not the Beast.* He paused for moment. *It was a long time ago.*

Kate looked at Weston, who shrugged and said, "He doesn't usually pick up on old crimes. This is something I haven't seen before—HEY!"

Kate turned. Christopher had jumped down, onto the sand. He was walking into the water. She could see the current pulling at the legs of his jeans.

"Stop!" she shouted.

Weston leaped down after him. He strode out into the water and grabbed Christopher by the arm. The boy made a low keening sound of protest and tried to pull away, into the river. Kate jumped down as well and started toward the water when Christopher suddenly stopped resisting. He let Weston drag him to the bank.

Weston was almost breathless. "What the hell were you thinking, boy?"

I... don't know. Christopher sounded dazed, like someone suddenly awakened out of a deep sleep. *Please don't be mad at me.*

Weston let him go. "I'm not mad," he said softly. "You just scared me, is all."

"Scared both of us," Kate said.

I'm sorry. I'm sorry. He sounded close to tears.

"It's okay," Weston said. "Let's get back to the car. Maybe it's cooled down some."

3

WHEN THEY CAME OUT OF the woods near the road, there was a battered green and white pickup truck parked behind the SUV. A slender young man in ripped and faded jeans, a white T-shirt, and ball cap was standing by the Rambler, peering through the driver's side window. Weston quickened his pace, and Kate fell in behind, checking to make sure Christopher was following.

The man straightened up and waved as they approached.

"Hey," he said. "Y'all havin' car trouble?"

He looked to be about seventeen or eighteen. He had a long, pale, angular face that might have been handsome if not for the pathetic attempt at a mustache and goatee that covered his upper lip and chin in ragged tufts. His straw-blond hair stuck out in several directions from under the ball cap, which Kate could now see read GIT 'ER DONE.

"Overheating," Weston said.

The young man nodded. "Shit happens," he said, then he blushed and ducked his head. "Sorry, ma'am."

My God, Kate thought, he's actually blushing.

"Not a problem," she said, and smiled at him.

His blush deepened. He turned to Weston and cleared his throat. "Why'nt ya let me have a look at her?"

"You a mechanic?" Weston asked.

"I do a little work for my cousin sometimes. Don't often get to look at a classic like this one, though. What is she, a '65?"

"'64," Weston said as he raised the hood again.

The young man peered beneath it. He tentatively tapped his fingertips against the radiator cap as Weston had, then quickly pulled them back.

"Yow," he said. "Hot as a two-dollar pistol." He bent down and looked the engine over more closely. "I dunno for sure, pardner, but I think you might have you a cracked water pump housing." He pointed. "Look there."

Weston grunted a reluctant agreement. Kate stuck her head up under the open hood. She had no idea what she was looking at.

"How much will that cost to fix?" she said.

The young man stepped back. They stepped with him. He slammed the hood shut. "Don't know, ma'am, I don't even know how to go about gettin' parts for somethin' this old. But Poodie'd know."

"Poodie?"

"My cousin. He runs the garage in town." He nodded with pride. "If Poodie can't fix her, she can't be fixed. And I ain't gonna bet against him."

"Well," Kate said, "I guess we need to get it... her... to Poodie's."

"Tell you what. I'll lead y'all into town and Poodie can send the tow truck back. Y'all can at least wait indoors."

"We don't want to be any trouble."

"No trouble at all, ma'am. I work for Poodie. I just need to... whoa."

Kate turned to look at where the young man was staring.

Christopher was standing by the front of the SUV, his attention fixed on something across the road. Kate followed the direction of his sightless gaze. It was then she first noticed the mailbox and the driveway beside it. The box was nearly overgrown with creeper vine and the driveway was only in slightly better shape. Christopher was staring at the driveway as if he expected something awful to come roaring out of it and onto the road.

"Where'd he come from?" the young man said.

"He's with us," Weston told him.

The young man looked dubious. "He okay?"

"He's fine," Kate said.

Weston was already moving. He knelt down beside Chris and took his hand. He whispered something in the boy's ear that Kate couldn't hear. Christopher shook his head.

"Hey, little man," the young man called out. He pointed at the boy's pants, which were still dark with moisture up to the knees. "You been swimmin'?"

"He went in the river," Kate said.

The young man shook his head. "Don't wanna be

doin' that. Not there. Fast water there, and deep, too. We lose someone ever' couple of years to the river."

"That's terrible."

"Yeah," he said and gestured toward his pickup. "C'mon, hop in. I'll take you folks with me up to Clyde's."

"I thought his name was Poodie."

"Got to pick Clyde up first," he said and nodded toward the driveway.

Christopher was still staring at it. Weston put a hand on his shoulder and he shook his head.

"Nothin' to be scared of, little man," the young man called.

Christopher didn't speak in Kate's head, but she could feel his unease. The boy clearly wasn't comfortable with the idea of heading up that driveway.

"Can we... just wait here?" she said. "You get your friend and we can follow you in my car on your way out."

The young man looked puzzled, but nodded. "Sure," he said, and stuck out his hand. "My name's Griff, by the way. Short for my last name. Griffin."

The awkwardness and shyness were back.

She took the hand and shook it, firmly. "Kate Messenger." She nodded toward Weston and Chris. "My friends there are Noah—he's the older one—and Christopher."

Griff raised a hand. "Hey again."

Weston just nodded. Christopher didn't seem to notice.

Griff turned to Kate. "Is Christopher, ah, you know..." he whispered and touched his ear, an eyebrow raised.

"He can hear. Quite well. He's not retarded, he's not autistic, and he's not stupid. He just doesn't speak."

"Sorry," Griff said. "I didn't mean to offend nobody."

He looked so forlorn that Kate backed off.

"It's okay," she said. "Thanks for your help. Go get your friend and we'll be getting our stuff out of the car."

"Okay." He slid behind the wheel. "Back in a sec."

As Griff drove the truck up the overgrown driveway and out of sight, Kate went over to kneel by Christopher.

"What's wrong?" she asked softly.

I don't know. Something's not right.

"Is something bad up at that house? Is *he* here?"

Christopher didn't answer.

She looked at Weston, then at the driveway. "Should we have gone with that young man?"

"If the Beast is here," Weston said, "Christopher would know it." He opened the door to the Rambler and pulled out the keys. "Come on. Let's get our gear moved. We may be here a while."

4

WESTON HAD THEIR SPARSE LUGGAGE—a duffle, Chris's suitcase, and a battered backpack—out of the Rambler and in the cargo compartment of the SUV by the time Griff came back.

He was alone in the truck. He pulled out onto the hard road, stopped, and let his passenger window down.

"Where's your friend?" Kate asked.

Griff's brow was furrowed with worry. "He ain't home."

Kate and Weston looked at one another. Kate felt a sense of foreboding. "Did you look inside?"

Griff nodded. "Yeah. Got the spare key from under the... from where they leave it. He ain't there. Maybe he caught a ride in early with Tara."

He looked up the road, then back at Kate.

"That's his wife. She's got the only car. She goes in early to work, but he don't usually go with her. He..." Griff trailed off. "He don't go in with her," he repeated lamely. There was obviously a story there that Griff didn't feel right telling to strangers. "Anyway, y'all follow me."

As Kate got behind the wheel of the SUV, she noticed

Weston had his sketchpad out. She stole a glance in the back seat at Christopher. He was staring straight ahead, and as she watched, he began a slow rocking back and forth.

She looked back at the road and pulled out to follow Griff, glancing from time to time at Weston, who'd begun drawing, bent over the pad, his eyes intent on the paper in front of him.

She still didn't understand the strange connection the boy and Weston had, the perfect... well, telepathy was the only word for it, that let Weston's hands draw the pictures Christopher saw in his head. But so far, she'd only seen it happen in connection with violent crimes, the kind of crimes that Christopher could feel the lingering echoes of.

"Was there..." she began after a moment, then realized Weston couldn't hear her. He always seemed to go away in these moments, possibly to the same place Christopher went.

She shut up and drove.

Griff's battered pickup led them down the narrow, cracked country road. A faded metal sign by the roadside said SINGER 2 MI, and Kate figured Singer was the town where they were headed.

After another mile or so, the road rose slightly above the surrounding land. It was then she began to catch glimpses of the river, glistening and sparkling through gaps in the trees.

The little convoy rattled over a small metal bridge that spanned a creek leading into the river.

At the other end of the bridge was a hand painted sign, cracked and faded with age. Above the words WELCOME TO SINGER, Kate could barely make out the painted sun rising—or maybe setting—over a blue river lined with trees.

A few wooden houses, as faded and worn as the sign, lined the road. Young children playing in a fenced-in yard stopped to stare as they passed.

They came to a four way stop. Kate glanced to the right and saw that the river was crossed by another metal bridge, much larger than the first. To the left was a small wooden church, marked with a freshly painted wooden sign:

ST. MICHAEL'S CATHOLIC CHURCH

Smaller letters underneath provided a translation: *Iglesia Católica de San Miguel.*

A young Latino man in khaki pants and a T-shirt was pushing a mower over the grass of the church's tiny side yard.

Griff stopped and waved out the window of his truck. The Latino man shut down the mower and walked over. The two men began talking.

"Okay," Kate muttered. "Can we move on? Maybe sometime today?"

She heard Weston let out a long breath and looked over.

He'd finished his drawing.

"Let me see," she said.

Without speaking, he turned the sketchpad toward her. She frowned. This was something different than she'd seen Weston/Christopher do before.

The previous drawings Weston had made had been seemingly random assortments of images: a hand, a picture of a ticket, a book. And eyes. Always the eyes. They'd been rendered with almost photographic precision. Weston, who claimed he couldn't usually draw a thing beyond stick figures, became a professional-quality draftsman under Christopher's influence.

This was something different entirely. The strokes were broad, sweeping, almost abstract. And they showed a complete scene. Kate could make out the river, and the outline of an unmistakably female figure kneeling beside it.

The girl's face was turned away, but Kate could see the sweep of long hair, almost touching the water. The trees beside the river arched over her, jet-black and menacing, ending in branches like grasping fingers.

No, not grasping.

Strangling.

Kate could almost feel the fingers around her own throat, and her hand went to her neck as if to stop it.

"What..." she began, but the word came out as a croak. She shook her head to clear it. "What is that?"

"I don't know," Weston said. He nodded toward the windshield. "He's moving."

She shook her head again and turned her attention back to the road. Griff was turning left. She followed him onto the main street of Singer, Alabama.

•

It was a small place, grown smaller and rendered near-ly a ghost town by times that started hard and only seemed to get harder.

Only a few of the businesses lining the broad two-lane main street showed signs of life: a hardware store with dirty windows, a small diner with its tattered menu taped to the inside of the front door; a building with a bright yellow, green and orange paint job that looked new. A banner draped across its front said MER-CADO MEXICANO.

But it was the building at the corner of the next block that interested Kate most. A large cinder block structure with three garage bays and a set of gas pumps out front. Behind the gas pumps was a glassed-in office.

The lettering on the glass identified the building as SINGER MOTOR FUELS AND AUTO REPAIR.

Griff pulled up in front of one of the garage bays. Kate followed, parking the SUV behind the truck.

As she got out, she heard Griff's voice calling, "Hey, Poodie! Poodie! Where you at, man?"

A fat man in stained dark gray khakis waddled out of a back room and into one of the bays. He wore an open dark blue flannel shirt over a tattered wife-beater tee. Unruly gray hair fringed his bald head, and his chin looked like it hadn't seen a razor in a few days. He regarded the young man sourly.

"You're late," he said.

"Sorry," Griff said. He motioned to where Kate and

Weston were standing. "Brought you some business, though."

The man looked doubtfully at them. "Hep you folks?"

"My car broke down on the road into town," Weston said. "We need a tow."

"It's an old Rambler," Griff said. "A '64."

"That a fact?" the fat man said. He arched an eyebrow at Weston.

"Yeah," Weston told him. "Your assistant here seems to think it's a cracked water pump."

Poodie's grunt let them know what he thought of Griff's diagnostic abilities. "I'll get the tow truck. Griff, you think you got time to watch the place, or do you have some other pressin' social engagements?"

Griff sighed. "I said I was sorry, Poodie."

"Sorry don't feed the bulldog, son." He turned to Kate. "You can wait inside if you like, ma'am. It's a little cooler in there."

Then he noticed Christopher getting out of the SUV. His face softened slightly from the sour visage that seemed to be his resting expression.

"Well, hey there, young fella."

Christopher raised a hand in greeting.

"Y'all go on in," Poodie said.

They followed him into the glassed-in office. A metal desk, covered with loose papers, parts catalogs, and a laptop computer nestled among them, took up about a third of the small space. A pair of chairs that looked cast off from someone's living room flanked a wicker table with a streaked and dirty glass top. There were a couple of old *Field and Stream* magazines and a *Reader's Digest* from 1983 on the table.

Poodie went behind the desk and took a key ring off a cork board behind it.

"Be right back," he said. "Hey, young man, you wanna sucker?"

Griff reached into a glass jar hidden behind a pile of catalogs and pulled out a small lollipop wrapped in cellophane. He walked over and pressed it against Christopher's palm. The boy smiled and nodded.

Poodie's brow furrowed. He looked at Kate. She shook her head while pointing at her mouth, and Poodie nodded his understanding.

"Okay, then," he said. "Let's go, Mister..."

"Weston. Noah Weston." He stuck out his hand. Poodie held up his own, filthy with grease, and smiled apologetically. Weston took it anyway and shook it. Poodie was still smiling as the two men walked out.

"Okay," Griff said, "Y'all make y'selves comfy."

Kate sighed and took a chair. Christopher took the other, unwrapping the lollipop.

Griff sat behind the desk and began tapping something on the laptop keyboard.

Kate picked up one of the magazines, which promised to teach her the best place to hang a tree stand. She put it down and picked up the 80's vintage *Reader's Digest.* She was halfway through an article asking "Can Social Security Be Saved?" when the door opened.

She looked up and saw the Latino man who had been

mowing the church lawn step inside. Up close, she noticed how good looking he was. His thick black hair was swept back from his forehead, and his features were strong and chiseled. She couldn't help noticing the way his muscular torso filled out his tight T-shirt. His presence in the small space reminded her of how long it had been since she'd been with a man.

Easy, girl.

"Hey, Griff." His voice was deep and well-modulated.

"Hey," Griff said. "Your Camry's ready. Let me ring it up."

As Griff shuffled through a pile of invoices on the desk, the man turned to Kate. "G'morning," he said. His smile looked like a movie star's.

She smiled back. "Morning."

"Dang it," Griff said and looked up. "I can't find the bill anywhere. And Poodie's out with the truck."

The man waved it off. "Not a problem. I'll come back."

"Sorry."

"Really, no problem. You ever find Clyde?"

Griff shook his head. "Nope. Has Tara heard from him?"

"No, and she's worried. And I was hoping he could help me with those gutters."

"I'll send him over if he turns up," Griff said, then grimaced. "And if he's sober."

"Whatever. Another day, maybe."

"Look," Griff told him, "go ahead on and take the car. I know you're good for it."

The man shook his head. "I don't want to get you in trouble with Poodie."

"Hey, Padre, if he can't trust a priest, that's his problem, ain't it?"

"Oh," Kate said out loud, then clammed up.

The man turned to her, still smiling. "Pardon?"

"Sorry. Didn't mean to interrupt. I just didn't... I mean..."

The man's smile grew wider, and there was a glint of mischief in his eyes as he said, "Let me guess. You thought I was the yard guy."

Now she felt the blood rush to her face. "I didn't... I mean..."

He laughed then. "Don't worry, I get that a lot." He stuck out his hand. "Esteban Morales," he said. "Sometimes known as Father Steve. I'm the priest at St. Michael's."

She stood up, still blushing.

"Kate Messenger," she said as she took his hand. "Sorry about the mistake, but, you know, you were out of uniform."

"Hey," Morales said. "You try mowing the grass in a clerical collar." He turned to Christopher. "And this young fellow is..."

"Christopher," she said as the boy stood up.

But as Morales took Chris's hand, something curious happened. The priest's arm shook slightly as if he'd received a mild electric shock. His brow furrowed as if he was puzzled about something.

"Christopher," he murmured. "Pleased to meet you."

He withdrew the hand and looked at Chris for a moment before shaking his head.

There was the roar and rumble of a large engine outside the window. The tow truck was pulling up, the Rambler secured behind it.

"Poodie's back," Griff said.

•

Poodie came in, with Weston following behind.

Poodie nodded to the priest. "Hey, Father."

"Hey," Morales said.

"So," Griff said. "I was right, wasn't I?"

"Let me have my chair back."

Griff got up. "Cracked water pump, right?"

Poodie slid into the chair. "Boy," he growled, "you are tryin' my patience."

Griff looked at Weston, who nodded. "Cracked water pump."

Griff's face split into a grin as he turned to Poodie. "I been lookin' up the part for you. Found a couple of places."

Poodie grunted as he stared at the laptop screen. "I got some good news," he said to Weston, "and I got some bad news."

"Give me the good news first."

"Good news is, I can get you the part, and it won't cost you an arm and a leg."

"And the bad?"

Poodie rubbed a hand over his stubbled face. "It's gonna take at least two days to get here."

"Two days?" Kate said.

Poodie shrugged. "It ain't somethin' they stock at Autozone. I can get a rush put on it, but I'm thinkin' a day and a half, two days, at least."

"What if we just sold the car?" Kate said. "How much would you offer for it?"

"It's not for sale," Weston snapped.

"Well, now," Poodie said, leaning back in his chair. "It is a classic, but not a popular one like, say, a Mustang or a Dodge Charger. Good condition, 'cept for the water pump..."

"It's. Not. For. Sale," Weston said.

"...but it ain't for sale," Poodie finished.

"Right," Weston said.

"If'n it was, though..."

"It's not."

"...I could give you forty-five hundred for it."

"We'll talk," Kate said.

"No, we won't," Weston told them. "Go ahead and order the part."

Poodie nodded. "Aiiight. Soon as I get Father Steve here his bill." He began tapping at the computer.

"I guess we need to find a place to stay," Kate said. "Are there any hotels around here?"

Griff shook his head. "The old Motor Court closed a couple years ago. Nearest one's up the road in Greenfield. About thirty miles."

Weston grimaced. "That far?"

"Sorry, man. This here's the ass-end of nowhere."

"You don't like it, Griff," Poodie said, "you can always leave."

"I didn't say I wanted—"

Morales broke in. "You folks can stay with me." They turned to look at him. "At the parsonage," he explained. "Behind the church. I've got a big spare room. And a comfortable couch."

Weston and Kate began talking at once.

"Oh, no, we couldn't—"

"Thanks, but we don't want to be any—"

He held up a hand to silence them.

"Part of the job," he said with that disarming smile. "Like the Book says. 'Be not forgetful to entertain strangers. For some have entertained angels unawares.'"

"We're not exactly angels," Weston said.

Morales laughed. "It's not required. And Tara—my housekeeper—is an excellent cook."

"That's for sure," Griff said, almost reverently.

Morales raised an eyebrow at him. "You want to come by, Griff, you know you're always welcome."

"Won't she mind unannounced guests?" Kate asked.

"She always makes way more than I can possibly eat. Really. I insist." He looked at Weston, whose mouth was compressed into a thin line. "And I promise. No sermons, if that's what you're worried about."

"I didn't say that," Weston told him, and now Christopher's voice came clearly to Kate.

We need to stay here.

She turned toward him, as did Weston. And, she was startled to see, the priest.

Morales smiled at him. "Did you say something,

young man?"

"He can't. Talk, I mean," Griff said.

Morales looked puzzled. "Really?"

As he turned back to them, Christopher "spoke" again. *We need to stay here*, he repeated. *There's something here. I feel it.*

This time, the priest didn't seem to notice.

"I think we're sold," Kate told Morales. "Noah?"

Weston only nodded. He didn't look happy.

Morales's smile widened. "Wonderful. Now, how much do I owe you, Poodie?"

Poodie handed him a piece of paper. "Two oh seven fifty."

"Not bad at all," Morales said. He took a checkbook out of his back pocket and borrowed a pen. As he wrote out the check, he told Weston, "Follow me. I'm in the beige Camry."

5

MORALES'S HOUSE WAS A SPACIOUS white single story wooden building that looked as if it had been built sometime around the turn of the twentieth century. A broad porch with white columns wrapped around the front and two sides. The paint job looked fresh. The hedges around the porch were immaculately clipped and the clean smell of newly cut grass filled the air.

The three followed Morales up the steps and across the porch to a door inset with leaded glass, next to a bay window. He entered without using a key.

"Tara?" he called.

A female voice answered from the back of the house as they entered a spacious front room that was big enough to serve as both living and dining area.

The furniture was old but comfortable looking. A long, brown leather couch faced toward the front bay window, with a pair of cloth chairs facing it to form a cozy visiting area. The couch divided the living and dining areas. A large rustic wooden dining room table filled the space behind it. Beside the couch was an old wood burning fireplace, swept as clean as the rest of the room. A simple wooden cross decorated the wall above the mantelpiece. There was no TV.

"Home sweet home," Morales said.

As he did, a young woman came into the room. She was small-boned and delicate looking. She had wide blue eyes that would have made her look childlike had it not been for the careworn wrinkles around them. She was dressed in jeans and a simple white blouse. Her thick blond hair was bound up in a kerchief atop her head.

"Hey, Father, did you find..." she stopped as she noticed Kate, Weston, and Christopher standing in the doorway. "Oh. Hello."

"Tara," Father Morales said, "this is Noah, Kate, and the young man is Christopher."

She gave a shy smile and a nervous wave. "Hey."

"Hi," Kate replied.

"Their car broke down and they're stranded," Morales went on. "It may be a couple of days before they can get the part to fix it. I offered to let them stay here. Do you think we could get them fed?"

"Oh," she said. "Sure. No problem." Her brow furrowed. "I may need to run up to the Piggly Wiggly for some more stuff, though."

"Take my car," Morales said. "Give the new tires a workout."

She smiled. For a moment, it made the lines around her eyes and mouth seem less pronounced. "Okay." Her face turned serious. "Ummm... did you see Clyde?"

Morales shook his head. "Griff said he wasn't at the house."

Her shoulders slumped. "Oh." Then she sighed and

looked up, a different smile plastered to her face. Kate could see the act of will behind that smile. "Oh well," she said in a bright, brittle voice. "I reckon he'll come home when he gets hungry. Like an ol' dog."

"Tara..." Morales began.

"Can I get the keys? I need to get to the store, then get started on supper."

Morales handed them over. "I'll be back in a minute," he said. He looked at Kate and winked. "I need to get back in uniform."

Tara watched him go as he walked into one of the bedrooms that opened onto the main room. She looked back at the new guests. "Pork chops okay with everybody?"

"Fine," Kate said. "Let me know if there's anything I can do to help."

She'd seen the look in Tara's eyes. She wondered if Father Morales knew his housekeeper was in love with him.

Tara headed out to the store, stuffing a wad of bills she'd retrieved from a drawer in the kitchen into her purse. Morales closed his bedroom door. When they heard the shower running, Kate turned to Christopher, who was sitting on the couch.

"Okay, kiddo. You said we need to stay here. What's up? What's so important about this place?"

I don't know. It just is. I feel it.

Weston retrieved the sketchpad from the luggage and opened it. "Does it have something to do with the drawing we did?"

Maybe. I don't know.

Kate took one of the chairs. "What about *him*? The Beast?"

He's been here. I can... I can smell *him.*

Kate and Weston looked at each other, then back at Christopher.

"Here?" Kate said. "In this house?"

Christopher shook his head. *No. Around.*

"But he's gone now?" Weston said.

Christopher just nodded.

"How long?" Weston asked.

Not long.

Weston persisted. "Then why is it important that we stay?"

I don't know.

"Was he at that house?" Kate asked. "The one where Griff went?"

Maybe.

Kate sighed. "This isn't really helpful, Christopher."

"Just be patient," Weston said. "Give it time. Maybe we should do a gathering."

He was referring to the process by which Christopher collected images and impressions before transferring them to Weston's sketchpad.

Kate frowned. "At that house? I don't know if—"

"Ah, that feels much better," Morales interrupted as he came into the room. He'd exchanged the white tee for a more conventional priest's black slacks, shirt and clerical collar. He was drying his thick black hair with a fluffy towel. A gold cross hung from a chain around his neck. "If anyone feels like a shower, I've left towels in the bathroom, and I'm pretty sure I haven't used up all the hot water."

Kate stood up. "A shower sounds fantastic."

"Great," Morales said. "I figure you two can take the guest room, and if Chris doesn't mind, he can bunk down on the couch."

Kate cleared her throat. Weston looked embarrassed. Neither one answered.

The priest frowned. "I say something wrong?"

"We're not married," Kate told him. "Or, you know. Together. Not like that."

"Not anything like that," Weston said, and Kate felt a flash of annoyance at the vehemence in his voice.

Morales slung the towel around his neck. "Ahh. Well." He pondered for a moment. "Then I guess, Kate, you can have my bed, Noah can take the guest room..."

"I'm not putting you out of your bed," Kate said.

"Me either," Weston added.

Morales raised a hand to quiet them. "I sleep on the couch all the time. Especially when I'm reading. It's no trouble. And Chris, we've got some cots in the church basement. The Boy Scout troop uses them when they go camping. Would that be okay?"

Christopher's smile and energetic nod indicated that this would not only be more than okay, but actually be pretty cool. Kate smiled as well. It was good to see the usually somber boy act like a kid again.

"Well then," Morales said, "that's settled. Kate, can you and Chris help Tara out when she gets back? Noah, maybe you can come with me to get the cot."

He walked out without waiting for agreement.

Weston glanced at Kate, then followed.

6

WESTON CAUGHT UP WITH FATHER Morales as he was crossing the street toward the church. He fell in quickly with the priest's long strides.

"So," Morales said, with elaborate casualness, "I have a feeling there's a story here."

"Kind of."

"Mind telling me?"

"Kind of."

They had reached the far curb. Morales stopped on the sidewalk that ran by the church and looked Weston in the eye. "Are you Christopher's father?"

Weston stopped and looked back, his gaze steady. "No. I'm his guardian."

"What does that mean?"

"It means his parents are gone. They abandoned him. I take care of him."

"So Kate's not his mother."

"No."

"Noah," Morales said, "I want you to tell me the truth. Did you two kidnap that boy?"

"No. And that's the truth."

"Are the three of you running from the police?"

"No. In fact, Kate used to be a police detective. Out

west."

"And what brings you here?"

"It's a long story."

"Maybe we can hear it over dinner."

"It's not exactly dinnertime conversation."

"Which brings me back around to being concerned. Are the three of you in some kind of trouble?"

"No."

"Noah, if you are in trouble, I swear to you I'll do everything I can to help you. But—"

Weston broke in. "Why?"

"Why what?"

"Why should I believe *you*?"

Morales ran a finger beneath the clerical collar. "Ummm... hello?"

"That collar's supposed to mean something to me? How do I know you didn't get stuck out here in the ass-end of nowhere, as that kid put it, because you got caught diddling choirboys? How do I know *you* can be trusted around Christopher? After all, it's not like he can tell anyone if you messed with him."

Morales's eyes narrowed and his jaw clenched. "I can forgive that. But only because forgiving is the business I'm in."

He got hold of himself with a visible effort. He closed his eyes and took a deep breath. His jaw relaxed and he opened his eyes.

"You're an angry man, Mr. Weston," he said in a calmer voice. "I don't think I've met anyone quite so angry. And I don't know why. It worries me."

"You want us to leave?"

"No. I just want to know you're not trouble. Or that that boy isn't in danger."

"You want me to swear before God?" Weston said. "You want me to swear on a stack of Bibles?"

"From your tone I get the feeling you don't put much stock in either of those."

"I don't. But I can't think of any other way to let you know how—"

Morales broke in. "What happened to your faith, Noah?"

Weston looked away for the first time. "What makes you think I ever had any?"

"Because only a man who's had faith and lost it speaks about it with that much bitterness."

Weston had no intention of telling him how right he was. He had never missed a Sunday at church before Anna and the girls were butchered.

He decided instead to tell Morales a partial truth. He'd found it more effective than a lie in deflecting inquisitive meddlers.

"My family," he said. "Christopher's foster family. Kate's mother. They were all murdered. Different times, different places."

The priest looked at him steadily, as if trying to decide if Weston was telling the truth. Then he put a hand on Weston's shoulder. "I'm sorry for your loss."

Weston fought down the urge to knock the hand away. "We met. We started talking. None of us had any roots left where we were. So we started traveling together. We... support each other."

"I understand," Morales said.

No, Weston thought, you really don't.

"We gonna get that cot now?"

•

By the time Weston and Morales had returned with the cot and set it up in the guest bedroom, the house was filled with the aroma of cooking. Tara had returned before them and had immediately gotten to work in the kitchen.

"Don't know what you're putting on those chops, Tara," Morales called out, "but it smells incredible. What's the secret?"

Kate was getting the flatware out to set the table. Her offer of aid in the cooking had been cheerfully turned down by Tara.

"I got it, hon," she said as she set to work. She seemed to have forgotten her earlier shyness and apprehension in the kitchen. She moved with the grace and economy of motion of someone doing something they'd done for years and loved every minute of it.

A radio set on top of the refrigerator was turned to low volume and tuned to the local oldies station.

Tara hummed along with it, occasionally singing a little snippet of lyric in a sweet alto voice. When the priest called out his compliment from the next room, Kate saw a broad smile break out on her face. Tara went in that moment from pretty to beautiful.

"Mama's secret recipe," she called back in a flirtatious sing-song. "I'll never tell."

Kate felt a stab of pity in her heart for the girl. There was no way this was going to work out well for her.

The premonition came true sooner than she'd thought it would.

Tara and Kate were putting the plates on the table when they heard a car pull up in the yard. Through the walls they could hear the blare and crunch of heavy metal guitar from a car stereo driven beyond its limits.

A slamming door, a peal of high pitched laughter, then the roar of a big engine as it drove away, taking the guitar with it. They all stood still, as if frozen, listening.

Kate could see that Tara's previous sunny mood had evaporated. She looked stricken as she slowly put the plate she was holding down on the table. There was the heavy tread of boots on the front porch. Something crashed against the door, causing Tara to jump and Father Morales to rise from his chair, frowning. Then someone was knocking on the door, hard and insistent.

"Tara!" a voice bellowed. "TARA!"

Morales threw his napkin down on the table and headed for the door, his face stormy.

Tara was faster, though, and intercepted him halfway across the living room.

"Please," she said in a low, urgent voice. "Let me handle him."

He looked at her for a long moment, and Kate saw something unspoken pass between them. Morales stepped back, but stayed a few feet inside the door, his arms crossed, as Tara opened it.

"Hey, baby," she said.

The man outside had been leaning on the door with one hand as he pounded on it with the other, and he nearly fell to his knees as she pulled it open. He stumbled momentarily, then pulled himself unsteadily upright.

"Hello, Clyde," Morales said.

7

UNDERNEATH THE TWO DAY STUBBLE and whiskey flush, Kate could tell that at one time, Tara's husband Clyde had been a good looking young man. Failure and alcohol had aged him prematurely. His dark hair was uncombed and greasy, a lock hanging down over his red-rimmed and bleary eyes. He looked as if he hadn't been to bed in two days and hadn't been sober for longer than that.

He squinted slightly as he looked at Morales, as if trying to figure out who he was.

"Hey, Father," he mumbled finally.

"Folks have been worried about you, Clyde."

Tara said, "Where you been, honey?"

Clyde swiveled his head toward her, then back to the priest, his face taking on the aspect of a bull trying to decide which one of the people in the room to charge. "Job interview."

"Hope it went well," Morales said. "Is this," he made a gesture that took in Clyde's appearance, "a celebration? Did you get it? The job, I mean."

As inebriated as he was, Clyde didn't miss the barely disguised contempt. He showed his own disdain by ignoring the question and turning to Tara. "You ready to go?"

"I was just getting dinner on the table," she said. "Wait a few minutes and I—"

"We're goin' now," Clyde told her.

"You're welcome to join us," Morales said. "There's plenty."

Clyde straightened up slightly. "*My* wife," he said in a low, hateful voice, "is gonna make me *my* goddamn dinner, in *my* goddamn house. If that's okay with you, *Father*."

"That's fine, Clyde. But I'll thank you not to take the Lord's name in vain in *my* house."

Kate thought Clyde might actually go for Morales at that point. His face got redder and she could see his fists clenching at his sides. She moved toward where Christopher sat at the table, determined to get him out of the room if the two men started fighting. When she saw the boy, however, she stopped.

His sightless eyes were fixed on the tableau across the room, his head cocked to one side, listening. He was practically quivering with alertness, like a bird dog on point. She slid to one knee beside his chair.

"What is it, Christopher?" she whispered. "What are you seeing?"

The Beast, he said.

"You're kidding," Kate blurted out. She couldn't help it. There was no reconciling the idea of that this wreck of a man was the one responsible for the savage butchery of so many—including her own mother. Besides, that murder had happened years ago when this guy was just a child. Hell, Kate had been barely more than that herself.

It's not him. But he knows the Beast. He's met him. I can feel it on him.

Clyde had apparently noticed the three people sitting at the table for the first time. He squinted again, trying to make them out through the fog. "Who th' fuck are these people?"

Morales started to say something, but Weston startled Kate by moving forward, hand outstretched, a friendly grin plastered across his face.

"Noah Weston," he said to Clyde. "Pleased to meet you."

If Kate was taken aback by the show of bonhomie by the usually taciturn Weston, it was nothing to Clyde's reaction. He actually stepped back, blinking in confusion at this grinning apparition who had suddenly thrust his way toward him.

He stopped, looked down at Weston's still outstretched hand. Then, slowly, as if he didn't quite believe it himself, he raised his own hand and shook Weston's.

"Looks like you been havin' yourself a time," Weston said, still grinning madly.

"Uh," Clyde said, and suddenly the tension was broken. He released Weston's hand and looked around, as if he'd just woken up and was unsure of where he was.

"We need to get you home," Tara said. "I'll get my purse." She scurried into the next room. In a moment, she was back. "Come on, baby. Let's get you home and fed, okay?"

Clyde frowned again.

"Nice to meet you," Weston said. "See you soon."

Clyde looked at him one last time, then followed Tara out the door.

The room seemed to let out its collective breath.

The smile dropped from Weston's face.

"What an asshole," he murmured.

•

They all made their way back to the table and sat down. Morales, who'd been looking pensive, seemed to recall his manners.

"Let's bow our heads for the blessing," he said in a subdued voice.

He did so, and so did Kate.

"Bless us, O Lord," Morales intoned, "and these your gifts, which we are about to receive from your bounty. Through Christ our Lord. Amen."

"Amen," Kate whispered out of politeness. She looked up to see that Weston was sitting there, head unbowed, his arms folded across his chest. The priest didn't seem to notice or, if he did, he made no remark.

They began to eat in uncomfortable silence.

Finally, Kate decided to speak up. "So, how did you come to be here, Father?"

That got a smile. "You mean, what's a Latino priest doing in a little lily-white town in Alabama?"

"Well, I have to admit, I was a little surprised to see a Catholic church here."

"Only one for miles around," he admitted. "So we get

the folks who don't want to drive all the way down to Mobile. And of course, the Latino community is growing. Especially during the spring and summer. Lots of migrant workers."

"Bet that causes some agitation," Weston said.

Morales sighed. "I wish you weren't right, Noah. We have two Masses on Sundays: the 8:30 and the 11:00. They seem to have self-segregated. The Latinos all come to the 8:30, the Anglos to the 11:00. I'd like to get them together. It might lessen some of the tension between the Latino community and non-Latinos."

"People like Clyde," Kate said. She wanted to get the priest talking about the young man after what Christopher had told her.

Morales shook his head. "Clyde's a good man. He's just going through a rough patch. He lost his job a few months ago and he hasn't been able to find another one. That makes what I pay Tara the only income coming into the house."

"That's got to hurt his pride," Weston said.

Morales nodded. "Yes."

And it doesn't help, Kate thought, that his wife's got a thing for her boss.

Morales went on. "They tried taking in a roomer for a while, but that didn't work out."

Kate and Weston exchanged a glance.

"A roomer?" she said.

"Yes. A man and his little girl. But they moved on after a while."

Weston put down his fork and leaned forward intently. "Why did they leave?" he asked. "They didn't get along or something?"

"I don't know," Morales said. "I think the father couldn't find the right facilities for his daughter. She was a special needs child."

He glanced at Christopher, then looked away.

"Special needs?" Weston asked. "Like Down syndrome?"

Morales looked surprised. "Yes. She had Down syndrome." He looked hard at Weston. "Do you think it might've been someone you know?"

"Maybe," Weston said. "Someone we met on the road. Do you know a name?"

Morales nodded. "Beaumont. Marshall Beaumont."

"No," Kate said. "That's not the guy we're thinking of."

Morales looked at her steadily.

She dropped her gaze to her plate.

"Not the guy," she said.

The priest didn't pursue the issue, and the rest of the meal passed in silence. Finally, Morales pushed himself back from the table. "Just leave the dishes in the sink. Tara always gets them first thing in the morning."

"No," Weston said. "I'll do them."

"You don't have to..." Morales began.

"It's the least we can do," Kate said. "Noah, I'll dry if you wash."

"Okay," Morales said. He stood up. "Look, I hate to leave you folks, but I do a 7:30 Mass every Wednesday for anyone who wants to come. It's usually only a couple of older folks, but—"

"Go ahead," Kate said. "We'll be fine."

"And this is the night I usually go to my study afterward and write the homily for Sunday. My sermon."

"I know what a homily is," Weston said. "Take your time."

"There's a TV in the guest room. Feel free to use it, or to read any of the books on the shelves. There's beer in the fridge. If you need anything—"

"You're across the street," Kate said. "You'd best get going, or you're gonna be late."

8

THEY MADE QUICK WORK OF the dirty dishes and cook-ware, as if they'd been working together for years.

"Did you hear what Christopher said?" Kate asked as she stacked the dishes in a plastic drying rack in one side of the double sink.

"No," Weston said, "but I saw him."

"He thinks that roomer that Clyde and Tara had—"

"Is the guy we're looking for. I got that. So we need to talk to her."

"We need to talk to Christopher first. Find out what he knows. What he's sensed."

"And whether that girl, that Tara, is in any kind of danger."

Kate paused. "I hadn't thought of that."

Weston smiled sardonically. "I thought you're sup-posed to be the detective."

She threw the rag down and walked out without answering.

Christopher was sitting on the queen-sized bed in the guest room, his unseeing gaze fixed on the TV. There was no cable, just a rabbit ear antenna on the back of the old set, which sat on top of a dresser with some of the drawer handles missing. They'd managed to pull in a station that was showing *Jeopardy!*, which seemed to make the boy happy.

"Christopher," Weston said. "Are you okay?"

Yes.

"Can we talk about what happened earlier?"

Sure.

Kate turned the TV down and sat on the bed beside him. Weston pulled over a faded brown armchair with stuffing poking through in places. He sat down. "Kate says you know the Beast was the one staying with those people."

And Lucy.

"And Lucy, yes. How do you know?"

That man, Chris said. *The one who came here. The Beast spent a lot of time with him. Like I said. I can feel it on him.*

Weston leaned forward. "What do you mean? How does it feel?"

I don't know. He's... different than he was.

"You mean Clyde? How do you know what he was like? You've never met him."

I just know. There's a part of him now... there's a part that's not him. *It's something the Beast left.* He paused. *And I think he left it for me to find.*

"Wait, what?" Weston said.

He knows we're coming. That we're chasing him. And he wants us to know he knows.

"Oh, my God," Kate murmured.

"Christopher," Weston said, his voice urgent. "What did he do to Clyde? Is that girl in danger? Right now?"

He's fighting it. He's trying. That's why he drinks. Because he thinks it makes the voice in his head go away. But the voice is getting louder. Christopher sucked in a breath that was almost a sob. *He's losing.*

"Okay, that's it." Kate stood up. "I'm going back out there."

Weston stood as well. "And do what, exactly?"

"Stop whatever's about to happen."

"You don't know that anything is."

"You heard Christopher. The man we're after—Bonner, Beaumont, whatever he's calling himself now—I don't know what he is. Maybe he's like Chris. He's got some kind of power. And he's had some sort of, I don't know, influence on Clyde. And knowing what we know, we can pretty much assume that that influence isn't a good one. Clyde's wife could be in danger."

She walked out of the guest room and into the living room where she'd left her purse.

Weston followed. "You're not a cop anymore, Kate. What are you gonna do if nothing's happening? Tell them, 'oh, sorry, the boy we're traveling with told me in my head that Clyde's possessed by the serial killer we're following'?" He stopped as she opened her purse and took out a nine-millimeter Beretta. His face darkened. "What is that?"

She took out a magazine and began sliding rounds into it. "It's a pistol, Noah. What do you think it is?"

"I told you, no guns."

"And I ignored you." She finished filling the magazine and slid it home. "What the hell did you think we're going to do when we finally catch this animal we're after? Give him a good scolding?"

Weston's voice rose. "So you're gonna shoot Clyde? For what you think he *might* do?"

Please, Christopher's voice rang in both their heads. *Please stop fighting.*

They turned. He was standing at the edge of the living room. He had his hands folded across his stomach as if it hurt. He was rocking slightly from side to side.

Please stop fighting, he said again.

Weston and Kate looked at each other.

"Okay," Weston said to him softly. "I'm sorry."

"Look," Kate said, "I'm just going out there to take a look. If there's nothing going on, I'll come right back."

"If you go out there, I'm going with you."

"Someone has to stay here with Christopher."

I can go, Christopher said.

"No you can't," Kate and Weston said at the same time.

You need me to go. To do a gathering.

"Not if there's a... if there's trouble," Kate said.

I'll stay in the car.

"No," Weston told him. "You're not going." He turned to Kate. "And neither are you."

"What are you gonna do, tackle me?"

"If I have to."

She held the gun up, pointed off to the side, finger outside the trigger guard. "You forget, I have the gun."

"So you'd shoot *me,* now?" Weston's voice rose.

"That's the problem with people like you, You think that goddamn thing gives you the right to—"

"Look, I'm not going to argue gun control with you right now. I'm—"

We're all going.

Christopher's voice had a timbre to it they'd never heard before, the steely finality of a jail door slamming shut.

Kate's mouth closed with an audible snap. Weston looked at the boy as if he'd grown a second head.

Enough talking, that steely voice came again. *We need to move.*

He walked to the front door, opened it, then turned around. His sightless eyes looked into the room between them.

Are you coming?

He didn't wait for an answer, just opened the door and walked out.

"What in God's name *is* he?" Kate whispered into the silence that followed.

Weston's voice was equally subdued. "I don't know. But I think we're following him."

9

THEY FOLLOWED CHRISTOPHER OUT TO the car, where he'd already opened the door to Kate's SUV and climbed into the back seat. Kate had stuck the now loaded pistol back into her purse, and fumbled awkwardly with it as she got into the driver's seat. She couldn't very well put it on the passenger seat as Weston climbed in, and she knew if she handed it to him, she might not get it back. It didn't feel right to put it in the back seat with Christopher.

Weston saw her discomfort and nodded. She hated the smugness in that nod.

"See?" he said. "Those things cause more problems than they solve."

"For god's sake, give it a rest," Kate said. "I need to put this on the floor by your feet. Just let it be. Okay?"

"Whatever."

She put the purse down and he got in.

The road out of town was not lighted, and the long summer twilight was fading, leaving only a soft purple glow in the horizon. From time to time, the headlights illuminated clouds of swirling white bugs, some of which ended their short lives spattered on their windshield. The window washer and wiper just smeared their remains into a thin paste across the glass until Kate stopped the car and pumped the windshield washer again and again.

"Jesus," she said, "how do people live here?"

Weston didn't answer. When she started moving again, however, he spoke in a quiet voice.

"My wife's daddy was one of the finest men I ever knew. He was one of the old time lumbermen. He could cruise a stand of timber and tell you within five dollars how much it was worth."

"Okay," Kate said. She had no idea where this was going.

"He set me up in the business. Lent me the money to buy the equipment for my first sawmill. No promissory notes, no terms, no interest rate, and no lawyers. All on a handshake. He said he knew I'd do right by him just like I'd do right by his daughter. He never once asked for a payment, but I paid him back just the same. Every dime. Took me ten years, but I did it. The day I made the last payment, he just smiled at me and said 'I never doubted you for a minute, son.'" Weston's voice caught in his throat. "I felt like I was ten feet tall that day."

"He... sounds like an extraordinary man," Kate said hesitantly.

Weston didn't seem to hear her. He spoke as if he was talking to himself.

"Three days later, he was having a beer with his workers down at the bar. He'd just closed a deal on the biggest tract of timber he'd ever bought, and they were celebrating. If he was gonna get rich, he was gonna share the happiness and the wealth. That's the kind of man he was. A couple of rednecks at a nearby table got into a tussle over something. I don't know what it was, something stupid. My father-in-law walked over and tried to calm things down. One of those bastards pulled out a gun. I guess he was trying to kill the guy he was fighting with, but he missed. He shot my father-in-law in the throat. By the time the paramedics got there, the finest man I knew had just finished drowning in his own blood. Shot by some dumb-ass drunk redneck who thought a gun was the answer to all his problems."

Kate was silent for a long minute.

"Noah," she finally said.

He interrupted her. "There's one more thing. When he died, my wife's daddy left her his favorite car. One he'd hung onto for decades."

"A 1964 Rambler."

"Yeah. He knew it was special to her. To both of us. See, that's the car Anna and I used to date in. I was just poor white trash, from up on raggedy-ass Weston Hill in Stokes County, and I couldn't afford a car any more than I could have flapped my arms and flew to China. But Freddy Wayne Jessup let me court his daughter, in his favorite car, because he saw something in me that I didn't even see in myself."

"And that's why you won't let the car go."

"Yeah."

"I'm sorry. I didn't know."

"No," Weston said, "you didn't."

Kate hit the brakes and yanked the car over to the

side of the road. Christopher made a sudden sound of alarm as he grabbed the handle above his door.

"You know *why* I didn't know?" she said, her voice rising. "Because you didn't tell me. You don't tell me *anything*." She slammed the car into park and stomped on the parking brake. "Look, I get it. The cops and the local DA had you pegged for your family's murder. They still do. You're pissed about that, and I don't blame you. But *I'm not them*. I'm on *your side*. I left my life and drove out into the middle of East Bumfuck on the strength of a message I still don't understand, delivered into my head like some kind of psychic Western Union from halfway across the goddamn country by a boy with powers I still have trouble believing are real—no offense, Chris."

It's okay.

"And I'm a little lost here, okay? I don't know how to navigate this. And you don't make it any easier, sitting over there all wrapped up in your anger and your distrust. If we're gonna be partners, I need you to tell me what's going on, at least from time to time. Would that be okay with you?"

Weston didn't answer. He stared straight ahead, into the cone of light made by the headlights of the SUV.

"We're partners?" he said finally.

"Well? What the hell else are we? I mean, the end game here is facing down some sort of vicious monster who kills families and cuts out their tongues. We may very well be doing it without any backup but each other. I'd like both of us to know that when the time comes, we'll have each other's back. Doesn't that seem like a good idea?"

"Yeah." Weston said the word as if it was being dragged out of him.

"Well, if you can't fully accept the idea, could you at least make a start? By not being such a judgmental asshole?"

Weston stiffened. "*I'm* the asshole here?"

Kinda, Christopher said.

Weston looked startled, then angry again. Then he smiled a rueful smile.

"Okay," he said. "Point taken." He rubbed a hand down his face. "I'll do what I can."

"Thanks." She pulled the car back out onto the road.

"I think we're almost there," Weston said.

We are.

10

KATE STOPPED OPPOSITE THE DRIVEWAY. "Noah, can you hand me my bag?"

Weston didn't know what to do. He didn't want to be there. He knew that Messenger's plan would lead to nothing but trouble, trouble they didn't need. He hated the idea of the woman going up that driveway, in the dark, toward God knew what.

But there was no way to stop her short of knocking her over the head and dragging her back to the priest's house. Noah Weston had never struck a woman in his life, and he wasn't about to start now. If she had to go, he'd be damned if he'd let her go alone.

But his first responsibility was to Christopher.

"Look," he said, "let me go. I'll go look around, come right back, and let you know. You stay here with Christopher."

She shook her head. "If you go, you're not going unarmed."

"I'm not taking a gun."

"Then I'm going. Now hand me the bag. Please."

Damn it, woman, he wanted to shout, but he bent down and did as she asked. He turned to look at Christopher in the back seat. The boy was sitting still, his head slightly cocked as if he was trying to pick up a faraway noise. "Chris, can you feel anything?"

No. A moment's pause. *There's too much noise. It's like static. And it's coming from the river.*

"The river?" Weston said. "Are Tara and Clyde down there?"

No. Something else.

Kate and Weston looked at one another.

Finally, Kate said, "I'll be right back."

Weston was about to try once more to reason with her, but Christopher spoke first.

Both of you go. Back each other up. I'll stay here. I'll be fine.

Messenger was already getting out. Weston shot Chris a glance, then shook his head and followed. He caught up with Kate and they started up the narrow driveway, side by side.

The clay and gravel crunching beneath their shoes was humped in the middle, cut with gullies to either side, and seriously needed to be gone over with a grader. Taking anything other than a vehicle with a four wheel drive up here was asking for a broken axle or worse.

Uncut vegetation encroached right up to the edge of the roadway and brushed against them as they made their way slowly up the path. Kate held her pistol down by her side, her finger outside the trigger guard.

A gnat whined in Weston's ear, then another. He brushed at them, only to have them come right back. Crickets and frogs in the woods on either side were making such a racket that Weston thought they could have led a brass band up here without anyone hearing their approach.

The slow walk seemed to take forever, but it was probably no more than fifty yards or so before Weston spotted the yellow glow of an outside light.

"I see it," Kate whispered as he raised a hand to point.

They drew closer, and the trailer came into view.

It was a single-wide, set up on concrete blocks at the four corners and in the middle. There was no under-pinning or skirting, so they could see right under the trailer. It stood in a cleared space at the end of the drive. The yellow bug light above the white metal door showed the rust stains on the trim and the place where one of the four panes in the small window had been replaced by a piece of cardboard. It was the only light on.

A red Ford Focus was parked by the wooden steps.

They stopped at the edge of the clearing. There was nothing moving and no sound but the frogs and crickets.

"Little early to be going to bed," Kate said.

"Well, Clyde was pretty wasted. Probably passed out. Meaning he's no danger to anyone."

Kate put her gun back in her shoulder bag. "I guess you're—"

Before she could finish speaking, the front door opened. They froze.

Tara was standing in the door, dressed in a tank top

and cutoff blue jeans. A large calico cat bounded out the door past her, then streaked away under the trailer. The girl began to close the door, then stopped. She leaned forward slightly, peering into the darkness.

"Hello?" she said. "Is anyone there?"

Weston saw Kate moving. He reached out as if to pull her back, but she stepped forward, to the edge of the circle of dim light.

"Tara," she called softly, "it's Kate Messenger."

Weston gritted his teeth and stepped forward as well.

Tara cast a glance back over her shoulder, then came down the steps, closing the door after her. She walked over to them, picking her way gingerly in bare feet over the gravel and packed dirt. "What are y'all doin' out here?"

"We got concerned," Kate said. "Clyde seemed a little angry. We wanted to make sure you were all right."

Tara looked confused. "Did Father Steve send you?" Her face brightened a little as she spoke his name. "Is he with you?"

"No," Weston said. "He's at the church. Writing a sermon." He couldn't help adding a little sneer to the last word.

"Oh." She looked down at the ground. "Well, you can see I'm okay." She looked back over her shoulder. "Y'all need to leave. If Clyde wakes up and finds you here..."

"Tara," Kate said, "Are you afraid of Clyde? Is he hurting you?"

The answer came too quickly. "No. No. He's not." Her eyebrows pulled down in anger. "And what th' hell business is it of yours, anyway?"

Weston broke in. "What about the other guy?"

Tara's growing irritation turned to bafflement. "What other guy?"

"The guy who stayed with you a while back."

"The one with the little girl," Kate said.

"Were you afraid of him?" Weston felt this turning into an interrogation, but he couldn't stop himself.

The frown was back, deeper this time.

"How did you know... did Father Steve..." she stopped and shook her head angrily. "Look," she said, "I got to do what I got to do when I'm working. But I'm off work. This is my house. An' I don't have t'answer any damn questions. From you or anybody. Now y'all git. Before I call the law."

Weston wanted to press on, but Kate spoke up first. "Okay," she said. "I'm sorry to have bothered you."

Tara didn't answer or look back as she walked to the trailer with long, angry strides, then went inside and closed the door behind her.

"Well, I guess that didn't go the way you planned it," Weston said.

"Shut up," Kate snapped. "Let's go."

When they got back to the car, Christopher was gone.

11

KATE STARED INTO THE EMPTY BACK seat.

"What...? Where did he...?"

"Goddamn it," Weston fumed. He slammed the passenger door and cupped his hands to his mouth. "Chris!" he bellowed.

Kate looked around frantically, trying to figure how long they'd been gone, how far the boy could have gotten.

Unless he was taken...

She felt the sensation of ice-cold hands twisting her guts at the thought. The moon was rising, throwing its cold light over the scene. She looked across the strip of vegetation toward the woods. She thought she saw something moving there, a flash of white through the darkness.

"Look," she said, pointing. "The woods."

"The river," Weston said grimly. "He said something about the river."

They were both moving then, Weston calling out "Chris!" as he broke into a run. They plunged into the tree line, Kate slightly behind Weston.

At night, the woods seemed less welcoming than they had earlier. The darkness seemed to close in all around, broken only here and there by the patches of white moonlight that made it through the canopy. She could barely see where she was going. The whisper of the slight breeze that stirred the cottonwood trees seemed filled with menace.

Then, at the edge of her hearing, as if from far away, she caught a sound. She couldn't make it out at first. It seemed to tickle the base of her brain, like a mental itch she couldn't scratch. As she stopped and listened, the sound became clearer.

It was a woman singing.

The song had no words, and no tune she could follow, but it filled Kate with an indescribable melancholy. It was a song of infinite loneliness and irrevocable heartbreak. Tears sprang to her eyes as the music became louder.

"Chris!" Weston shouted again.

The sound broke the spell, the music vanishing like a burst soap bubble. Suddenly, they were at the river bank. Kate stopped, teetering at the edge of the sharp drop that led down to the beach she'd seen earlier. Another inch, and she would have gone sprawling into the water.

Weston had dropped down onto the sand.

"Chris!" he shouted.

Then she saw Christopher. He was in the water, up to his waist, moving with determination toward the center of the black river. The fast moving current made ripples around his thin body. He stumbled slightly on the slick river bottom and Kate's heart leaped into her throat.

"Christopher!" Weston shouted, his voice cracking with anxiety. "Turn around, son! *Turn around!*"

He plunged into the water after the boy.

"CHRISTOPHER!"

Finally, Chris seemed to hear Weston's voice. He turned around, slowly, almost slipping again. He seemed disoriented.

Kate couldn't take any more. She kicked off her shoes and waded into the water, up to her knees.

"Come on, Christopher," she called out. "This way. Over here."

Weston was still pushing his way through the water, holding his arms out toward the boy. Christopher hesitated for a moment, then slowly began heading back toward the shore.

"That's right, son," Weston said. "Come to me. Come to my voice. That's it."

Her heart pounding, Kate watched them grow closer and closer. Then she saw something rise up behind Chris, a shadow blacker than the water, blacker than the night. Even the moonlight couldn't cast any illumination onto that figure.

She couldn't make out a face or any features, but the outline looked human. She heard Chris's voice in her head, more frightened than she ever had.

Noah. Kate.

Then his voice was drowned out by another—much louder—voice that seemed to come from the bottom of an endless well of rage and hatred, saying only one word.

MINE.

Kate's scream combined with Weston's shout as the shadow wrapped around Christopher, enveloping him in that unnatural darkness. Then it pulled him down, into the water, and they were gone.

Weston shouted again and dove after them, headed for the spot where Christopher had disappeared.

Kate waded deeper, then stopped. The voice she had heard had shaken her to the core. It had taken the heart from her. She didn't know which way to go, and every direction seemed hemmed in by terror. She was alone with the black river sliding by, that sinister whisper of the wind in the trees, and her fear. She stumbled and started back toward the riverbank.

To her left, a few feet away, something seemed to explode out of the water.

It was Weston, clutching Christopher to his chest. They were both gasping and choking, spitting water as Weston staggered toward the bank. The black figure was gone.

Kate turned and headed back into the water, reaching a hand out to Weston. As he grabbed her, clamping his hand so tightly to her wrist she cried out in pain, Kate heard the voice again.

MINE!

She sobbed in horror and despair as the shadow rose up again, less than three feet away. The smell of the thing made her gag, a fetid stench of rot and decay.

She yanked Weston's arm as hard as she could, feeling as if her shoulder was separating from its socket. She grabbed Christopher with her other hand as she pulled the two of them to her, then twisted her body to pull them around and put herself between them and the thing she could hear splashing behind her.

With a mighty shove, she sent them both toward the bank, then turned.

She wished more than anything in the world that she had her gun.

The shadow-thing loomed before her, seeming as large as an oak tree. She charged forward, throwing wild punches, knowing it was hopeless, knowing the thing, whatever it was, was going to envelop her, drag her down, take her to the bottom of the river. She only prayed that it would end there. That she would simply die, and not be kept alive somehow, in torment, for the amusement of whatever this evil creature was.

"Leave us alone!" she screamed.

Her fists connected with nothing. She went sprawling, onto her hands and knees in the shallow water. In a blind panic, she staggered upright, waiting for the creature to land on her back and bear her down into the dark, dark river, down to that rotting riverbed where she'd die with her lungs full of water and mud and things long dead. She turned, determined to die facing the thing.

There was nothing there.

The moonlight shone on the riverbank, illuminating the figures of Weston and Christopher. Weston was on his hands and knees, retching. The boy was lying on his back, motionless.

Kate splashed to the shore and went to Christopher. His sightless eyes stared up into the night sky, unblinking. He didn't seem to be breathing.

"Chris," she moaned in agony. "Oh, God, please no."

He looked so small. Weston knelt beside her, putting two fingers over the boy's carotid artery.

"I'm getting a pulse," he said, his voice strained and hoarse.

Christopher convulsed once and took a deep gasping breath. Then another. Then his breathing settled down to something approaching normal.

"Oh, thank God," Kate said. "Christopher. Talk to me, kiddo. Please."

Slowly, he sat up. She threw her arms around him, weeping with relief.

I'm okay, Kate. She's gone.

"She?" Kate said.

Chris turned that unnerving milky white gaze to Weston.

"Okay," Weston said, responding to something Kate hadn't heard. He got to his feet and bent to pull Christopher up with him. "We need to get to the car," he said to Kate. "I need the sketchbook."

"What?" Kate said. "No. We need to get him to a doctor. God knows what he may have breathed in."

I'm fine, Christopher said. *Please. This is important.*

He put his arm around Weston's waist for support and the two of them started walking back toward where Kate's SUV sat parked on the side of the road.

She watched them for a moment, baffled, then got up to follow.

Christopher put his other arm out, inviting her to help, and Kate took up her position on the other side.

The three of them slowly made their way back together, through the dark woods.

12

"ARE YOU OKAY TO DRIVE?" Weston asked when they reached the car.

"Yeah," she said.

She wasn't sure if that was true, but she got in anyway.

Christopher handed Weston the sketchbook and a pencil. There was an urgency about his movements until he settled into the back seat.

As Kate pulled away, Weston went into a trance and began to draw. Kate's clothes were still clammy from the river, and before long, the air conditioning had her shivering. She switched it off. Neither Weston nor the boy seemed to notice. For the moment, she may as well have been alone in the car.

By the time they reached the small bridge into town, Weston had finished. He sat back and let out a long, shuddering breath, like a man who'd just endured a painful field surgery without anesthetic.

"Let me see," Kate said.

"When we get back to the house."

Father Morales was waiting for them on the porch when they got there, sitting in one of the old rockers. He didn't get up as they pulled in and Kate killed the engine.

She turned on the interior light. "So show me."

Weston hesitated, then turned the sketchbook her way.

It was the same scene he'd drawn before, the long-haired female figure by the river, with the menacing trees arching overhead. But this time the girl's face was turned toward the viewer.

Kate gasped.

It was a face that would have been beautiful if it hadn't been contorted with rage and a malice so deep and disfiguring that it turned the woman into something fearful and hideous.

It was the face of a monster.

"Who is it?" Kate whispered.

"I don't know," Weston said. "But I think she's a little bit pissed off."

"Is that what attacked us?"

Yes, Christopher said, then he shivered, but not from the cold. *She's so lonely. That's why she's angry.*

Kate thought about this, but wasn't sure she wanted to. Not the way she was feeling right now.

"We need to get out of these wet clothes," she said, "before we catch cold."

The three of them got out and trudged toward the house. Morales watched them coming. He'd taken off his clerical garb and was dressed in jeans and a T-shirt. The gold cross around his neck remained, however, gleaming in the dim porch light.

He held a beer in one hand. As they drew nearer, he

regarded their bedraggled condition, concern in his gaze. "Is this another story you don't want to tell me?"

Before anyone could answer, he raised a hand.

"You'd better get changed, first. I'll put some coffee on. And some hot chocolate for you, Christopher, if you'd like some."

The boy nodded.

By the time Kate had changed into a pair of dry jeans and a blouse, the smell of coffee filled the house. Christopher was sitting at the table with his mug. Morales sat with him, looking at Weston's sketchbook.

"This is good work," he said. "Disturbing, though."

You have no idea, Kate thought.

"It's Noah's," she said.

As if summoned by name, Weston came out of the guest room, toweling off his hair.

"You've got a lot of talent here," Morales told him.

"Not really," Weston said, "but thanks."

Morales flipped a page. "I see you've heard of our local legend."

Weston sat down and gently but firmly took the sketchbook from the priest's hands. "What legend is that?"

"Wait while I get the coffee. How do you take it?"

"Black," Weston said.

"One sugar," Kate said.

Morales was back in a moment with three steaming mugs. The coffee was hot and soothing going down, and it warmed a part of Kate that she wasn't sure would ever be warm again.

"The town's called Singer," Morales began, "because of the legend. A long time ago, a young woman was waiting for her lover by the river." He smiled. "Some versions of the story say she was a Choctaw princess, but that can't be right."

"Why?" Kate asked.

"American Indians don't have princesses," Weston said. "That's only in Disney movies."

Morales nodded. "Exactly. But anyway, whoever she was, the girl supposedly had a beautiful singing voice, the most beautiful anyone in these parts had ever heard. As she waited by the river, she was singing a song. A man passing by heard her. Some versions of the story say it was her lover and they quarreled, others say it was..." he looked at Chris and stopped what he was about to say, "just a bad man. In any case, he killed the girl by the river. Strangled her, and threw her in. Or buried her. No one really knows. Just that her body was never found."

"Don't tell me," Weston said, "let me guess. To this day, people can still hear her singing by the river."

Morales smiled. "Right. As I said, the body was never found, so there she stays. And those lured in by her song are led to their doom. Pulled in by the girl in the river and drowned as revenge for the wrong done to her." He took a sip of his coffee. "But that's just an old ghost story. There are stories just like it around the world, or so I've read. The Russians call a spirit like that a *rusalka*."

"You seem to know a lot about it," Kate said.

"I read a lot." He took another sip and looked at them shrewdly over the top of his cup. "Ahhh," he said with satisfaction as he put down the cup. "Now that I've told you all a story, maybe you can tell me one. Tell me about your moonlight swim."

Kate could feel Weston's eyes on her. "We... got worried about Tara. So I wanted to go out and check on her."

"Those cop reflexes never go away, do they?" The lightness of the words contrasted sharply with the tension in Morales's voice.

Kate shot a look at Weston, wondering how much he'd told the priest about her. "I guess not."

"So," Morales said with the same transparently false casualness, "I assume she was all right."

"Yeah," Weston said. "She was fine."

Kate saw him relax.

"That's good." He looked at Kate. The look of appraisal was back in his eyes. "So how did you end up in the river?"

She found herself wishing he didn't have such nice eyes. She hated lying to him. Before she could say anything, Weston answered for her.

"Christopher wandered off," he said.

Morales glanced at Chris. "That's a very dangerous thing to do, young man."

Chris ducked his head as if to say *I'm sorry.*

Weston went on. "He was only going down to the river's edge. He likes listening to the water. But he fell in, and I had to—"

"He didn't fall in," Kate blurted out. "Something dragged him in." She took a deep breath, then kept going. "Something tried to drown him, Father. And Noah, too."

13

"KATE..." WESTON SAID.

She ignored him and kept her gaze on Morales. "Christopher was in the water when we got there. We called to him to turn around and come out. He tried. But someone—some *thing*—grabbed him. It pulled him down. Noah and I went in after him. We fought with it. Whatever it was."

"An alligator," Morales offered. "They take their prey right off the banks, drag it into deep water and drown it before eating it. We see gators in the river sometimes. Big ones."

Kate shook her head. "You see any bite or claw marks on him? This thing was... I don't know what it was. But it wasn't any alligator. It wasn't anything natural. It was *evil*."

Her voice was shaking. She picked up the sketchbook.

"*Look* at her! It's that thing you described. That... what do you call it... *rusalka*." She set the book back down with a sigh when she saw Morales's face. "You don't believe me."

"I believe you believe it," he said gently. "And thank you for being honest." He looked at Weston. "It's a refreshing change of pace." Weston looked away as Morales went on. "The important thing is that everyone's all right. Are you okay, Christopher?"

Christopher's blind eyes turned to the priest, seeming to study him for a long moment. Then Kate heard his voice in her mind.

I'm fine, Father Steve.

The priest blinked in surprise. "Wh... What did you just say?"

I said I'm fine. And you can trust Kate and Noah. They're my friends. They'll never hurt me.

It was the first time Kate had ever seen the priest shaken.

"*Madre de Dios,*" he whispered, then crossed himself.

Don't be afraid, Christopher said. *Tell him, Noah.*

Weston was shaking his head. He clearly regarded this as a bad idea.

It'll be all right, Christopher said. *He's a good man. He'll help us.*

Weston hesitated before beginning.

"Christopher has... a gift," he said. "He sees things that other people can't see. He feels things that other people can't pick up on. Mostly he can feel the aftermath of an act of violence. Like a killing."

"Like the murder of that girl," Kate said. "So many years ago."

Weston shook his head. "I've never seen him gather something from that long ago. That's what we call it. Gathering."

It's easier in the thin places, Christopher said.

Kate looked at him. "That's the second time you've used that expression. Thin places. What does it mean?"

"It's a term from Celtic mythology," Morales said. He looked numb, like a man trying to decide if he was dreaming. "It's a place where the barrier between this world and the next is thinner. More porous. It's where things come through from the—" he made air quotes with his fingers—'other side'." He rubbed his hand over his face. "This is crazy. It's old pagan superstition."

"Pot, meet kettle," Weston muttered.

"Stop it, Noah," Kate said and looked at Morales. "Whatever it is, it works. Those drawings are what Christopher sees."

"How can he... I thought Noah..." the priest pushed his chair back from the table. "I need to think about this."

He stood up.

"We're using Christopher's gift," Weston said, "to try and track down the man who killed my family. And the people at Christopher's group home. And Kate's mother."

"And we also think he might have been here," she said. "Recently."

"Beaumont," Morales said without hesitation. "Clyde and Tara's houseguest."

Kate nodded. "Christopher says he might have had some influence on Clyde. And that's the other reason we went out there. To see if we could find some trace, some trail, that would help us catch the Beast."

"That's what we call the killer," Weston said. "And

Father, we don't think he stopped with my family. In fact we know he hasn't. He's killed again, and he wants to kill more. We're always a step behind him, but if we can get a step ahead, maybe we can stop him. For good."

Morales was shaking his head. "I need to think about this. I need to pray. I need to ask the Lord for guidance."

"Yeah," Weston said. "Good luck with that."

Morales acted as if he hadn't heard him. "I'm going to the church. I don't know when I'll be back. Go ahead and lock up. I have my key."

As he reached the door he turned back and looked at them for the first time since Christopher had dropped his bombshell.

"Not every gift is of God," he said quietly.

Then he was gone.

•

Weston sat and watched the closing door. Then he turned to Kate. "Well, that cat's out of the bag."

It'll be okay, Christopher said. *He'll help us.*

Weston grimaced. "If he doesn't decide you're some kind of demon."

He won't.

"I hope you're right. And that he doesn't come back with a Bible and a vial of holy water. Or a shotgun."

Kate stood up. She hadn't realized how tired she was. She actually swayed a bit.

"I'm going to bed," she said. "I need to sleep."

"Sweet dreams," Weston told her.

She frowned. "I hope no dreams at all. Not after what happened tonight."

14

KATE GOT HER WISH.

She slept all night without dreams and awoke to the sun shining through the window and the smell of brewing coffee.

Through the bedroom door, she could hear the sounds of people moving around the house. She swung out of bed and pulled on a pair of jeans and a T-shirt.

Father Morales was standing by the couch, folding a blanket. His face was slack with fatigue and his eyes were rimmed in red.

"Good morning," he said, his voice slightly hoarse.

"You don't look like you got very much sleep," she said. "I'm sorry. I put you out of your bed."

He offered her a tired smiled. "I wouldn't have gotten much sleep anyway. I spent most of the night at the church."

Weston came out of the guest room, buttoning his shirt. "And what did God have to say?"

The priest sighed. "He seems to be content to let me work this out myself."

"We gave you a lot to digest last night," Kate said. "I'm sorry."

"If what you've told me is true, what you have to

bear is worse than what I have to digest."

"It's true," Weston said. "But it's not your—"

At that moment, Tara came out of the kitchen, a plate in either hand. "Breakfast is ready."

She didn't look as if she'd slept much either. But the thing that struck Kate was that she was wearing a long-sleeved blouse with a high collar. It looked far too formal for cooking and cleaning.

Kate looked at Weston, who nodded his understanding.

"Let me help," she said as she headed for the kitchen.

"I got it," Tara murmured. "Y'all just sit."

Christopher came out of the guest room. He stopped and cocked his head, in that listening attitude that had become familiar to Kate. Then he walked to the table and sat down.

The rest took their places as Tara brought more plates, filled with scrambled eggs, strips of bacon, and buttered toast. Morales took his seat last, and Kate saw that he had noticed how Tara was dressed as well. His face darkened with anger.

"Tara," he said.

"Anyone want coffee?" she asked. Without waiting for an answer, she disappeared into the kitchen. A moment later, she was back out, carrying a glass coffee pot. She began pouring the delicious-smelling brew into Morales's cup first.

"Tara," he said again.

"Kate, Noah? You want coffee?"

"Sure," Kate said softly. "Thanks."

"Smells great," Weston said.

By the time she got to Weston's cup, however, her hands were shaking so badly that half of the coffee slopped out and into the saucer. He had to shove his chair back quickly to keep from getting splashed.

"Sorry," she said. "S-sorry..." then her composure broke. She banged the coffee pot down on the table and fled into the kitchen.

Morales leaped up and followed her. Kate started to get up, but Weston gestured for her to stop.

"Let them be for a minute," he said quietly.

Through the kitchen door, they could hear the sounds of Tara weeping as if her heart would break.

After a moment, Father Morales came out of the kitchen, his arm around her. The young woman staggered a bit in his grip as the priest guided her past the dining table and into the living room. He sat her down on the couch, still beside her with his arm around her heaving shoulders.

Kate tossed her napkin down and went to them. She got down on one knee in front of Tara and took her hand.

"Tara," she said.

The young woman looked up. Her hair hung in disarray about her tear-streaked face. "Leave me alone," she sobbed. "Just leave me alone."

Kate was insistent. "Can you roll up your sleeves for me?"

Tara shook her head, but Morales reached down and gently, almost tenderly, unbuttoned her right sleeve. As he pulled it up and away from her wrist, Kate drew in her breath.

The finger marks on her forearm were red and swollen and would turn into dark bruises within the day. There were deeper indentations, filled with drying blood, where fingernails had dug in cruelly.

Tara reached up with her free hand and unbuttoned her blouse at the top, and pulled it open. There were more fresh bruises on her neck.

"There," she said, her eyes full of pain and anger. "Now you know. You happy?"

Her voice broke on the last word, and she collapsed to one side, burying her face in Morales's shoulder.

Kate stood up. "We need to call the police."

"No!" the word burst out of Tara as if torn from her throat.

She leaped up, pulling away from Morales, and tried to grab Kate.

"No!!" she screamed again. "You *can't!*" She began flailing at Kate, still sobbing hysterically, shouting with each ineffectual blow. "It's. Not. Your. Business."

As Morales stood up and took her by the shoulders, Kate tried to fend her off without grabbing her wrists and bruising them further. "Okay! Okay! No police unless you say so. I promise."

Tara collapsed back into Morales's arms like a puppet with its strings cut. He took her back down to the couch and wrapped her up in his embrace.

He looked up at Kate. "Just let her alone for a bit. We'll talk when she's ready to talk." He nodded toward the table. "Your breakfast is getting cold."

Kate didn't know what to do. She looked at Weston, who shrugged and sat back down at the table.

They passed the rest of the meal in silence, the only sound Tara's slowly diminishing sobs and Morales's soft murmurs to her.

Weston ate quickly, his face grim, like a man getting an unpleasant chore done. Christopher picked at his food. Kate couldn't get down more than half the meal, although it was delicious. Finally, she pushed her plate away.

"I'll wash this time," Weston said.

That got Tara's attention.

"No," she said from the couch. She stood up, wiping her red-rimmed eyes. "That's my job."

Weston took out a bandanna-sized handkerchief out of his hip pocket and got up to meet her.

"Here," he said gently but firmly as he handed it to her, "blow your nose and have a seat. We won't be long."

Tara hesitated, but the authority in Weston's voice brooked no opposition. Kate had a sudden vision of him as a father, and she felt a pang in her heart as she realized what a good one he must have been.

She followed him into the kitchen. They washed and rinsed the dishes in record time.

"Let the pans soak," Weston said.

Kate nodded.

When they returned, Tara had moved to the dining area. She was sitting with her elbows on the table and her head down. Morales had pulled his chair around beside her, talking to her in a voice so low that Kate couldn't hear.

Christopher sat across from them, his face impassive. Weston took the seat at the head of the table, where Morales had been sitting.

Family meeting.

The words popped into Kate's head unbidden, and she stifled a smile.

"So," Weston said to Tara in that same steady tone, "Clyde did that to you. Put those bruises and those marks on you."

Tara looked up. Her lower lip trembled as she nodded.

"And it's worse than the last time he did something," Weston went on, "and that was worse than the time before that."

She nodded again. "He ain't really a bad—"

Weston interrupted. "He's not a bad man. I believe you. But you know, sure as anything, that the next time's gonna be worse. Until he kills you."

She shook her head. "No. No, he'd never—"

"He will, Tara," Kate broke in. "That's how these things always go."

"This ain't one of 'these things'," Tara flared. "This is my damn *life!*"

"Tara," Morales said.

She sank back into the chair like a sullen teenager. "Sorry I cussed, Father."

"It's not that. You know they're right."

"I just met you, young lady," Weston said, "and I hardly know you at all. But I hate to see anyone hurt. And I'd surely hate to hear you got killed."

She looked up at him, her eyes wide, as if measuring his sincerity. He stared straight back at her. Then she looked back down at the table. A single tear fell onto the wood and she wiped at it with one finger.

"I hear Clyde didn't used to be like this," Weston said.

She shook her head again. She spoke so softly that Kate could hardly hear her. "He didn't. He was always so sweet."

"What happened?" Kate asked.

Tara shrugged, still looking down. "He lost his job. He started drinkin'. But even then, he was okay. I mean he was depressed, but he was okay."

"And then someone came into your lives," Kate said.

Tara looked up. "How'd you know..." she stopped, her shoulders slumping. "Yeah."

"Beaumont," Kate said.

"Clyde said he needed a place to stay. An' he had money. I didn't like the idea at first. You seen the trailer. There ain't a lot of room. But Clyde said he'd only be there a couple weeks. An' that little girl of his was so sweet. Even though she was, you know, retard-ed."

"Down syndrome, right?" Weston said.

Tara wiped her nose with the handkerchief. "I guess."

"So what happened?"

"They started spendin' a lot of time together. Beau-mont and Clyde. I don't know where they'd go. Clyde said they were lookin' for work, but they never found any." Her voice turned bitter. "Sure didn't seem to have any trouble findin' liquor though." She twisted the handkerchief in her hands, as if her slender fingers were looking for a neck to wring. "They went fishin' sometimes. They'd take their poles an' a cooler down to the river and stay all day. I'd have to take the little girl to work with me."

"I remember," Morales said. "Sweet, happy little thing. What was her name? Lily?"

"Lucy," Tara whispered.

Lucy, Christopher said in Kate's head at the same time, her heart rate accelerating a few beats.

Morales looked at her. "Are you okay?"

"Yeah," Kate lied.

"You look like someone just walked over your grave."

"I'm okay, Father."

Weston continued. "The river. They ever catch anything?"

"Sometimes. Not often. Most often they'd just come home drunk. An' Clyde started to... change. He got mad easier. An' always at me. Like it was my fault times were so hard for him." She shivered. "Sometimes he'd be sittin' on the couch with him, that Beaumont fella. I'd be in the kitchen and look over an' Beaumont would be whisperin' somethin' to him, and Clyde would be *lookin'* at me, with this awful expression..." Her voice was trembling.

Kate tried to steady her. "So when did Beaumont leave?"

"A week ago," Tara said. "I was about to tell Clyde he had to go. We didn't need the money that bad. But one day Beaumont just up an' left. I got up, an' he an' Lucy were gone. But that just seemed to make Clyde madder. He said I was the one that drove him away, an' now we didn't have that money or any other way for him to drive out an' look for work." She was getting teary again. "But he always seemed to get someone to pick him up, someone he an' Beaumont had met out drinkin', I guess. He'd say he was out lookin' for work, but he kept comin' home drunk. And mad."

Kate took a deep breath. It was time for the big question. "So what happened last night? I thought he was passed out."

"He was," Tara said, "When y'all were out there. But he woke up in the middle of the night." She was trembling again. "He was like some kind of wild man. He started yellin' an' grabbin' at me. He said..." she stole a look at Morales and fell silent.

"What did he say, Tara?" Morales asked.

"He accused me of messin' around on him. He said I was cheatin' an' he had proof."

"Cheating with who?"

She looked him in the eyes. "With you, Father."

There was a moment of silence as they looked at each other. She broke the gaze first and turned to Kate. "He knew you'd been there. I don' know how. I'da swore he was out..." her voice caught in her throat, "out like a light. But he... he knew." The words were coming harder now and her trembling grew worse.

"He said I better not be talkin'... talkin' to strangers. He... he held me down. He had a knife."

Kate felt a coldness in the pit of her stomach. "What did he do?"

Tara's composure broke again. She was sobbing, the words spilling out of her mouth as the tears ran down her face. "He... he said... he said if I kept runnin' my mouth, he was gonna cut out my tongue."

15

NO ONE SPOKE FOR A long moment. The only sound in the room was Tara's sobbing.

Finally, Weston leaned forward. "Let me get that straight. He said he'd cut out your tongue."

Tara just nodded.

"Had he ever said anything like that before?"

She shook her head. "He'd never threatened me at all. I swear, it's like someone's took him over."

"Someone may have," Kate murmured.

Tara stared at her. "What?"

Kate looked at Weston and he nodded. "Might as well go ahead and tell her."

"Tara," Kate said, "there's a reason the three of us are together. The man who stayed with you, the man who called himself Beaumont, may be a man we've been looking for. The last name we know him by is Michael Bonner."

Bonner was the security guard who had "found" the body of Kate's mother. But now, thanks to Christopher, they knew that had been a lie.

"Looking for?" Tara said. "Why?"

"Because he killed Noah's family. And Christopher's foster family. And my mother." She paused. "After he kills people, he cuts out their tongues."

"At least we hope it's after," Weston said.

Tara's eyes widened. "You mean I had... some kinda *serial killer* in my..." she stopped and shook her head again. "Wait a minute. That's crazy."

Honey, Kate thought, you have no idea. "Did he have a tattoo on the inside of his wrist?"

Tara blinked. "Yeah."

"A circle with a dot in the middle of it?"

Tara's hand went to her mouth. "Oh, my God."

"That would be a yes," Weston said.

"That's our man," Kate told her. "That's the guy we're after."

Father Morales spoke up. "If you've never met him, how do you know..." he looked at Christopher. "Oh."

"Chris is the only person we know of," Kate said, "who's survived an attack by this man. We call him the Beast."

Tara looked at Christopher. "Is that why he can't talk? Because this guy cut out his tongue?"

Christopher nodded. He started to open his mouth to show her the place where his tongue had been, but apparently thought better of it.

"This is crazy," Tara said again. "You're tellin' me my husband is... *possessed*? By some kinda travelin' serial killer?"

"Maybe not possessed," Kate said. "More like influenced."

Tara looked to Morales. "Can't you help him?"

"If you're talking about an exorcism, it's not that

simple," he said. "You need permission from the Bishop, a psychiatric examination to rule out—"

Weston interrupted him. "Where's Clyde now?"

Tara wiped her eyes. "I don't know. After he... after he threatened me, he got this look on his face. It was like he didn't know where he was for a minute. Then he just let me go, got up and left."

She tried to hand the handkerchief back to Weston, who motioned for her to keep it.

"He left walking?" he asked.

Tara nodded.

"Where would he go on foot?" Kate asked.

"I don't know. Maybe he called one o' his drinkin' buddies to come pick him up."

"Can we go to the trailer?" Weston asked. "To look around?"

Tara looked puzzled. "What good is that gonna do? Beaumont's gone."

"Maybe he left something behind."

Tara shrugged. "I guess. But he took everything he had with him. He didn't leave nothin'."

Weston smiled. "You never know."

•

They made the trip in silence. Kate drove as Tara sat next to her in the passenger seat, worrying at a ragged nail with her teeth.

Weston sat in the back with Christopher, his sketch-pad on his lap. He could hear Kate talking to Tara in a low voice. The words came indistinctly to him, but he could get the gist: what you're about to see may seem a little strange, but just let it happen.

It was a lesson Kate herself had been learning since Christopher had led them to her. It was the lesson *he'd* had to learn when Christopher had sought him out, then summoned him from hundreds of miles away to come pick him up.

Sometimes Weston thought that if he hadn't been dedicated to drinking himself into oblivion in the aftermath of the murders of his wife and children, he would have checked himself into a loony bin when he heard the boy's voice in his head. But he'd heeded the call, and now so had Kate.

Kate.

He was still uncertain as to how he felt about her. He'd had no use for cops since the Stokes County sheriff's detectives had blamed him for the vicious killing and mutilation of Anna and his girls. When they'd found out he'd been gone from the home because he'd been with another woman, they'd stopped looking at anyone else. When the woman had given him his alibi, they'd let him loose, but they'd still never looked any further.

That thought still brought the blood to his face and made his fingers curl into fists whenever it occurred to him. He also resented the way Kate did things, *changed* things, without consulting him. Things like telling the priest and his housekeeper about Christopher and about their quest.

He had determined in the months he and the boy had been together that they would fly as far under the radar as they could manage and attract no attention.

That woman, as he still called her in his mind, seemed determined to tell the whole damn world about what was going on. But Christopher had been firm in his resolve to keep her in their group, and he still trusted the boy and his strange gifts.

The other thing that unsettled him, if he was honest with himself, was that Kate Messenger was a damned attractive woman, and it had been a long time...

He ruthlessly pushed that thought aside. It would be a betrayal of his wife's memory to become involved with someone else. There was the boy to consider. It wouldn't be proper. And besides, he didn't even like her. Not much. And he was sure she didn't much like him.

He glanced over. Christopher was still, without the gentle back and forth rocking that indicated he was getting ready to begin gathering the psychic traces left behind in the wake of violence and death.

As if sensing his gaze, Christopher turned his blind eyes to Weston.

"You okay, Chris?"

Christopher gave him a smile and a thumbs-up. Weston smiled back. Even though he knew the boy couldn't see him, he had a feeling the message got through.

They were all silent from there on out, but Kate broke it as, a few minutes later, they pulled into the overgrown driveway of Clyde and Tara's trailer and brought the car to a stop.

"Okay," she said, "let's do this."

Weston found a blank page in his sketchpad as they all climbed out. Tara moved ahead and opened the trailer door, then stepped aside as they all moved past her into what could only generously be called a living room.

"Excuse the mess," she said.

Weston waved her off, led Christopher to the center of the room just feet from a tattered couch, then stood with the pad and pencil in hand as he waited for Chris to do his thing.

As if from far away, he heard the gentle *squeak* of the cheap wood beneath the carpet as Christopher looked toward the ceiling and began his rocking.

Weston felt a haze descending over his mind.

Are you ready, Noah?

He heard the boy, but his own voice didn't seem to want to respond, so he just nodded.

Then his mind went away.

16

"WHAT'S HE DOING?" TARA ASKED.

She stood in the doorway of the trailer, watching Weston as his pencil moved swiftly over the sketchpad's page. Christopher stood with his hands by his sides, continuing his slight rocking motion.

"Drawing," Kate said.

"I can see that. What's he drawing? And what's wrong with the boy?"

"It's kind of complicated. Can you show me the room where Beaumont and the little girl were staying?"

Tara entered, as hesitant as if she were walking into a lion cage. "This way."

She led Kate toward a narrow hallway, away from the kitchen and dining area that shared space with the living room. There were two small bedrooms down that hallway, one slightly larger than the other. Each room had a twin bed, made up, with a small bedside table. There was no other furniture. Several cardboard boxes had been stacked in a corner of the larger room.

"We was gonna fix 'em up when we had kids," Tara said. "But..." her voice broke, "I don't know if that's ever gonna happen."

"It could still happen," Kate told her. "Don't give up

hope."

Tara said nothing, but her face indicated that that ship might have already sailed.

Kate entered the larger room and sat down on the bed. "Is this the one Beaumont used?"

Tara nodded.

Kate looked around, trying to pick up some vibration, some lingering impression from the evil they were chasing, the way Christopher did. She felt nothing. It was just a room.

She looked over at the boxes. "What's in those?"

"Nothing. Just some old stuff. Books and old magazines, mostly. Been meanin' to donate 'em, but I never got to it."

Something made Kate get up and walk over to the stack of boxes. The top flap of one was loose and unsecured. She opened it and looked inside.

As Tara had said, she found a stack of old *Us* and *People* magazines. Resting on the top, however, was a black and white composition book, the kind commonly available in the school supplies section of any drug store.

A single word was written in the white space on the cover.

LUCY.

She picked it up.

"Hey," Tara said, "What's that doin' in there?"

"The little girl must have left it behind."

Kate opened the book, and what she saw there hit her like an electrical shock. She felt her knees go weak for a moment and almost dropped it.

Her own face stared up at her, rendered in pencil in the same almost photo-realistic style as the drawings Weston did from Christopher's visions. Beneath the picture, someone had written, in the same shaky hand as the name on the front:

HELLO KATE.

Her hands felt as if they belonged to someone else, fumbling at the page before turning it. The next one featured a picture of Weston, rendered with the same fidelity.

Tara had walked up behind her and was looking over her shoulder.

"Wow," she said. "Who knew that little girl was such a good artist? Maybe she was one of them, what do you call it, retarded kids that's really good at numbers or the piano or stuff like that."

"Savants," Kate whispered. "And that happens with autistic children, not ones with Down syndrome."

She turned the page again. Christopher's sightless eyes gazed back at her. Under his portrait was the dot-in-a-circle symbol the Beast wore on his wrist.

"So this guy, this killer—he knows you three?"

"It looks like he does," Kate said. "Or at least the little girl, Lucy, does."

She closed the book, her hands shaking.

Christopher was right, she thought. They know we're coming. They knew we'd be here. She left this for me to find.

"Are you okay?" Tara asked. "You look like you seen a ghost."

"I'm fine." Kate held up the book. "Can I take this?"

"I guess. Are you sure you're okay? Can I get you a glass of water or a Coke or something?"

"No," Kate said, regaining some of her composure. "I'm all right, really. We need to check on Noah and Christopher."

When they returned to the living room, Weston was sitting on the couch, rubbing his temples. Christopher was slumped in a chair across from him.

Kate was dying to show Weston what she'd just found, but wanted to wait until they were clear of Tara.

"Did you get anything?" she asked.

"Nothing that makes any sense," Weston said, his voice thick with fatigue. "Pictures of the river, mostly."

"Remember what Christopher said earlier? 'There's too much coming from the river.'"

Tara broke in. "What do you mean, 'what he said earlier'? He can't talk."

"He gets his meaning across," Kate said. She reached for Weston's sketchbook. "Let me see."

Tara's eyes were narrowed in suspicion. "There's somethin' you ain't tellin' me."

Kate didn't answer as she flipped through the sketchbook. As Weston had said, the last few entries were pictures of the river. They managed to capture the brooding and sinister effect of the dark, fast water. There was no picture of the thing that had attacked them earlier. But she noticed something in the corner of one of the pictures, a long view that showed the river through the trees.

She looked closer. "We need to get down there."

"Where?" Weston said.

"The river. Clyde's there. And he's in trouble."

"What?" Tara said.

Kate turned the picture so Weston could see. He squinted, then grimaced. "I don't get it. What do you see that I don't?"

"Just trust me on this. He's there." She turned to Tara. "Call EMS. Now. Tell them to get to the river."

"What? What the hell... if Clyde's in trouble, I'm goin' with you."

"No," Kate said. "Call EMS. Then stay here to guide them down there."

Apparently Weston hadn't needed any further prompting. He was already headed outside. "Stay here, Chris. Wait for us."

Kate followed him out the door.

17

WESTON WAS HEADED DOWN THE driveway at a fast jog that allowed Kate to catch up with him.

"What if... that thing's down there?" she panted as they ran.

"Don't... go in the water," he said, almost as out of breath as she was, but looking as if he'd die before he'd admit it.

As they neared the river, they found Clyde face down in a patch of fern, under the trees a few dozen yards from the water.

Kate gingerly rolled him over. He'd vomited before he passed out, and apparently fallen into the puddle and tried to crawl. The viscous pale orange fluid streaked the front of his T-shirt and jeans and dripped from his chin.

She turned away and retched at the smell.

Weston clenched his jaw and knelt by Clyde. He slid two fingers against the young man's neck. "He's got a pulse. Barely. And he's breathing, but I don't like how slow it is."

"What happened?"

Weston looked around. Then he reached back into the thick vegetation and pulled out a bottle. There was a bare half-inch of brown liquid sloshing around in the bottom of it. The dark orange label bore the picture of an elderly man and lettering in an antique font: OLD GRAND-DAD.

"Offhand, I'd say this happened."

Kate grimaced. "He's drunk."

"He's more than drunk. He's got alcohol poisoning. We don't get him to a hospital, he's gonna start seizing. Or stop breathing." He slapped Clyde across the face, hard. "Clyde. *Clyde*! Wake up, son." He slapped him again. "Come on, wake up."

Clyde moaned and shook his head, eyes still closed. Weston slapped him again, harder.

"Noah," Kate said, "don't beat his brains in."

Weston ignored her. He shook Clyde savagely, his teeth clenched. "Come *on*, damn it!"

Suddenly, Clyde opened his eyes. They were wide and panicky, with broken veins showing blood-red. He squirmed as if trying to get out of Weston's grasp, then clutched at him like a drowning man.

"Don't," Clyde wheezed. "Don't let me..." his stomach began to heave.

Weston barely got the young man's face turned away before he vomited again, staining the vegetation further.

Kate couldn't take it. She stumbled a few feet away, leaned against a tree, and lost what little breakfast she'd eaten. When she straightened up, she noticed the trail of broken fern and weeds where Clyde had stumbled and crawled to where he'd eventually fallen. It seemed to come from upriver.

She frowned. Where had he been?

She turned back and saw Weston cradling Clyde in his arms. "Stay with us, son. Try and stay awake."

"Don't let me..." Clyde said again, his breathing ragged.

"We're not going to let you die, " Weston told him.

"NO!" Clyde cried, then reached up and grabbed the front of Weston's shirt. "*Don't let me hurt her.*"

"Hurt who? Tara? You're not going to hurt her. You love her. Right? More than anything."

"I do," Clyde sobbed. "I do. I'd rather die than hurt her."

"Then why..." Kate began, but stopped as Clyde twisted out of Weston's grip and slid to the ground. He lurched up to his knees, then rose to his feet, tottering like a rotten tree in a high wind. "Water." He staggered forward. "River."

Weston sprung up beside him, steadying him with an arm around his shoulders. "Whoa, there. You aren't going swimming right now. Not in the shape you're in."

"Got to..." Clyde heaved himself forward again, arms outstretched like a zombie. His eyes burned with the desire to get to the water. To the river.

Kate looked where Clyde's gaze was fixed. She saw a ripple, as if something large was moving in the depths. She suddenly had the mental image of a big cat, crouched in tall grass,watching its prey, its tail twitching.

Waiting.

"Clyde," she called to him. She went to his other side and shored that up as best she could with her own arm. "Clyde. Look at me."

The young man's head swiveled slowly to look at her. She saw madness in those bloodshot eyes, but also the desperate and helpless pain of a man losing his mind and unable to stop it.

"Don't listen to her," she said. "You hear me? *Don't listen to her*. The woman in the river. Or to the other voice. You know the one I mean. Don't listen."

"I... can't..." Clyde's knees gave way and he sank to the ground. His chin fell to his chest.

"He's out again," Weston said.

In the distance, they heard the wail of sirens, growing closer.

•

They sat side by side on hard plastic chairs in the waiting room of the ER.

Christopher sat a couple of feet away, listening to the latest headlines from Fox News as they blared from the TV on the wall. He swung his legs back and forth, back and forth, scuffling his shoes on the linoleum worn from decades of feet.

The tiny rural hospital didn't have a cafeteria, so they were sating their hunger on crackers and sodas (Diet Pepsi for Kate, Cheerwine for Weston) from the vending machines down the hall.

"How'd you know he was there?" Weston asked her.

"It was in your drawing," she said. "Or Christopher's. However you describe it. You can see the figure lying in the grass."

Weston had brought the sketchbook in with him. He opened it to one of the drawings of the river. "I still don't see it."

She squinted. "It's... I..." she shook her head. "Let me see another." There was nothing there, either, just the water and the trees. "I could swear I saw it."

"Maybe you did, but not in the drawing."

They both looked at Christopher.

"He knew about it," Weston said.

"We should ask him," Kate said. "And about this."

She'd brought the composition book from the car and handed it to Weston without further explanation. She watched his face as he opened it. At first he went blank with shock. Then he slowly closed the cover and looked at the name before opening it back up again.

"Where did you find this?" he asked.

"At the trailer. In a cardboard box. In the room where *he* was staying."

"But the name on the book says 'Lucy.'"

"And those drawings are almost exactly the same style as the ones you and Christopher do."

He looked down at the book again. "I don't understand."

"Neither do I. But Noah, I think Christopher was right. The Beast knows us. He knows who we are."

"Or she does. Or they both do."

"Either way, they know what we look like. Our names."

Weston closed the book and handed it back, looking

a little dazed.

She took it from him. "I don't understand why this was left for us. Is it a warning? A taunt?"

"You assume it was left for us."

"Of course I do." Kate held up the book. "Didn't you see it? 'Hello Kate'? That was supposed to be found. By me. Which means—"

"He knows we're coming," Weston said with a nod. "I've wondered about this before. That house in Tacoma. The one he set on fire. I thought he might be trying to cover his tracks." Weston gestured toward the door leading to the rooms in the back where the doctor was most likely pumping Clyde's stomach. "But now I'm wondering... what if he's leaving traps for us? Obstacles to slow us down."

"You think that's what Clyde is? An obstacle?"

Weston rubbed his hands over his face. "I don't know. Maybe the guy just likes spreading the evil and misery around."

"You know what else this means," Kate said.

"Yeah. This... freak we call the Beast may not be ordinary. I mean, besides the killing. He may be different. Gifted. Like Christopher."

"Like us."

Weston flared. "He's nothing like..." He caught himself and the anger subsided. He looked as if he'd aged twenty years. "Yeah. Like us."

"It might not be him," Kate said. "Lucy could be the one with the power."

"The transmitter. With the Beast as the receiver."

Kate drew in a breath, then pitched her voice low, hoping Chris couldn't hear. "That means that sweet looking little girl..."

"Could be the real monster," Weston finished for her.

They thought about that, then Kate said, "Noah, have you ever wondered if Christopher knows more than he's telling us?"

"I can almost guarantee it. Don't forget he didn't tell me about you until I'd spent a night in one of your jail cells."

Kate nodded. "We need to talk to him."

"Here? Now?"

"Might as well."

Weston sighed. "Okay. Let me take the lead. He trusts me."

Kate felt a brief flash of resentment.

You mean *you* trust *him,* she thought.

Weston started to rise. As he did, the outer door to the waiting room slammed open and Father Morales strode in.

He was dressed in jeans and a T-shirt, without the clerical collar. His hair was uncombed. He looked about the waiting room for a moment before he saw them. He hesitated, then squared his shoulders like a man who'd decided on a course of action before walking over to them.

"Where is she?" he demanded in a voice hoarse with stress.

18

WESTON WAS THE FIRST TO answer. "She's with her husband."

With that reply, the priest seemed to deflate. His shoulders sagged and the set of his jaw relaxed.

"Yes," he said in a more subdued voice. "Clyde. How is he?"

"Not great," Kate said, "but they think he'll pull through."

"That's good," he told her, without conviction. He sank into one of the hard plastic chairs. For a moment, he was slumped, leaned forward, head down, elbows on his knees. Then he took a deep breath and straightened up. "And Tara?"

"She's fine," Weston said, "considering."

Morales nodded. "Good."

Weston stood up. "Father, can I talk to you for a minute?"

The priest looked up at him, his eyes bleak. "Sure."

Weston led the way to the area by the vending machines, with Morales following. He looked back into the waiting room, where Kate was trying to find something else on the TV for Christopher to listen to.

He turned to Morales. "Look. I know how you feel

about that girl."

Morales wouldn't meet his eyes. "I'm concerned about someone who—"

"Cut the bullshit, Father. A man would have to be blind, deaf and dumb not to see the way you look at her. And the way she looks at you."

Morales started to say something, but then closed his mouth. Finally, he spoke in a low, bitter voice. "You want to mock me."

Weston stayed expressionless. "Why would I want to do that?"

"Because you're right. I love her. I'm in love with my housekeeper. I'm supposed to be above that."

"I have to confess," Weston said, "I had a mind to mock you. But now, I find I just don't have the heart. Especially with you being honest and all."

Morales barked out a humorless laugh. "Thank the Lord for small favors."

"Also, we haven't got the time. There are some forces at work here. You need to get your mind right and focus on that."

"What do you mean, 'forces'?"

"Come on, Father. You know exactly what I mean. There's something that's trying to turn Clyde bad. Make him hurt people. Even people he loves. There's also something weird in that river. Something Clyde was trying to get to. I think he wanted it to kill him, because then he wouldn't hurt Tara."

Morales was shaking his head. "This is crazy."

"Are you saying you don't believe in evil spirits? In a

Devil?" Weston had lost his patience. "Because let me tell you, Father, I've seen what a devil can do. I've walked in the blood a devil spilled, blood soaking into the floor of a man's home. *My* home, as a matter of fact."

Morales gave him a tired smile. "So you believe in Satan but you don't believe in God? You realize the logical conundrum there, right?"

"I know I've seen more of the Devil's work than God's in this world. But let's get back to the problem we have right now."

"The problem I have now is that I need to, as you put it, 'get my mind right.' I'm supposed to be a man of God. And I'm failing Him. I need to confess my sins. I need to pray."

"And exactly what the *hell* good is that going to do?"

"If everything is as you say, and there are actual demons involved here, how am I supposed to face them, in a state of sin as I am?"

"You don't need to be all pure in heart to do what has to be done here."

"And what is that, exactly?"

"Get that girl away from here. Away from *him.*"

"Run off with her, you mean." Morales shook his head. "You know I can't do that. It's a betrayal of everything I believe. Besides, why can't you do it?"

"Because it's a distraction to us," Weston said quietly. "This is a stumbling block put in our way by the man we're after."

"You really believe that?"

"Kate found a book at Tara's trailer. It belonged to that little girl. Lucy. It had pictures of us. Pencil drawings. He *knows* us."

The priest blinked. "How...?"

"I don't know," Weston said. "Maybe I'll ask him when we catch up to him. But he, or that child with him, left that book so we'd find it."

"That's impossible," Morales said.

"I've seen a lot of impossible things lately. Every damn one of them weirder than the last. But I think that man, the one we call the Beast, he poisoned Clyde's mind somehow, made him dangerous. He knew we were coming. Maybe he figured Clyde, crazy as he was, would take us out."

"Think about what you're saying, Noah. He'd have to be able to predict you'd stop here. He'd have to know you'd stay with me. He'd have to be able to predict the future."

Weston's head was starting to hurt. He rubbed his temples as he said, "I don't know, Father. Like I told you, I'm not sure just what he can and can't do. Other than butcher people. But first things first. You need to get Tara away from Clyde. Someplace safe."

"If I do that," Morales said, then paused.

Weston read the look on his face. "You don't know if you can trust yourself."

"No. I *know* I can't." He took a deep breath. "I'm sorry, Noah. I can't be with her. Not now. Not ever. I made a vow, and as tempted as I am, I'm going to keep it. For my own soul's sake." He started to walk toward the lobby, then turned back. "There's one possibility you haven't thought of. Something that would explain the book, and how this... beast you're chasing would know where you'd be."

Weston felt the chill at the base of his spine as the import of the priest's words sank in. "You think—"

"Maybe he's still here," Morales said. "And he's watching you."

PART TWO

"Sometimes you find yourself in the middle of nowhere, and some-times, in the middle nowhere you find yourself."

~Unknown

19

KATE LOOKED UP AS MORALES walked back into the waiting room. He stopped by her chair and fished a key out of his pants pocket.

"I'll be at the church," he said, handing her the key. "After that, I may be gone for a few days. You can keep using the house until you get the car fixed."

"Wait, *what*? Where are you going?"

"If you need to move on before I get back, leave the key under the rock by the front porch steps."

"What about your congregation?" Kate asked.

"I'll call the bishop," Morales said. "They'll find a substitute."

"And what about Tara?"

"She has her own key. I'll tell the church secretary to keep paying her as long as she keeps coming to clean up."

"That's not what I mean and you know it. She needs you."

Morales shook his head. "I'm the last thing she needs."

Weston walked up to them. "He's running," he said contemptuously.

Morales didn't take the bait. "You're right. I am. I'm

running. I'm running from a woman, so you can add that. Because if I stay I'll ruin her life. And mine. And everyone's."

He turned and walked away, heading for the waiting room door.

A moment later he was gone.

Weston sank into the chair next to Kate. She saw the expression on his face.

"What?" she asked.

"Before he cut and ran, I told Morales about what we'd found. He brought up something that probably should have occurred to us."

"What?"

"Unless he's some kind of soothsayer, what's the one way that Bonner, or Beaumont, or whatever his name is, could know we'd be at Tara's? Or at the priest's?"

It slowly began to dawn on her.

"He didn't move on," she said. "He's still here."

"Somebody's been driving Clyde around. Maybe it's him. And that's why Clyde's getting crazier."

Kate glanced over at Christopher. "Looks like it's time we had that talk."

She raised her voice so the boy, who seemed engrossed in an episode of Adventure Time on the Cartoon Network, could hear.

"Chris? Could you come here a minute?"

At that moment, however, the doors to the waiting room opened and Tara walked in. Her face was streaked with tears and her hair hung limply around her face.

Kate and Weston jumped up and met her halfway across the waiting room.

"They're lettin' him go," she said, her voice still hoarse with grief and shock. "They're just turnin' him loose."

Kate couldn't believe it. "*What?*"

"The doctor said they ain't got any reason to hold him. They say he's just drunk."

"Goddamn it," Kate said.

The doors to the ER made a sound like a pistol shot as she burst through them.

An African American nurse in blue scrubs sitting behind a desk looked up in alarm as she blew past it.

"Ma'am," she said, leaping up, "you can't go back there."

Kate rounded on her. "I need to talk to the doctor who treated the young man who was just brought in here. The one with alcohol poisoning."

"That would be me," a voice said.

Kate turned.

A short, balding guy in pale green scrubs and stethoscope stood behind her, holding a clipboard. He had the pallor of a man who spent most of his time awake under fluorescent light and the tired, cynical eyes of someone with an incurable case of compassion fatigue. It was a look Kate had seen a lot of in her time on the job.

Burnout, she thought. She'd seen it in EMTs, medical examiners, social workers, and her fellow cops. She had little patience with it.

"Are you seriously releasing him, Doctor...?"

"It's Mister, actually," the man told her. "Mr. Tyrell. I'm a physician's assistant."

"What?" Kate said. "Why hasn't he seen a doctor?"

Tyrell glanced down at the clipboard, began writing something on it. "And your relationship with the patient is...?"

Kate fought down her anger at the tone. "My friend and I brought him in. He was unconscious. He was suffering from alcohol poisoning. How can you just turn him out like this?"

"Mr. Stouffer isn't a candidate for admission," Tyrell said, and began to turn away.

Kate realized that she hadn't known Clyde and Tara's last name. It made her slightly ashamed, and the shame stoked her anger.

"Why?" she said. "Because he doesn't have insurance?"

Tyrell turned back. "That's part of it, yes. He's also capable of being managed at home. I've given him some Ativan for the shakes, and some information about substance abuse rehabilitation options."

"He was trying to kill himself," Kate snapped. "And talking about hurting his wife!"

Tyrell arched a pale eyebrow. "He didn't mention anything about that. Neither did his wife, who he seems to have a good relationship with."

"Well, I heard him mention it. And so did my friend."

"Really?" Tyrell said. "What were his exact words?"

"He said..." Kate stopped.

"Said what?" Tyrell persisted.

Kate felt her shoulders slump. "He said, 'don't let me hurt her.'"

"Ah. So he was trying *not* to hurt others."

"We're playing word games," she said. Then she remembered what Tara had told her earlier. "He threatened to cut out her—his wife's—tongue."

Tyrell shook his head. "I specifically asked her if her husband had threatened or harmed her. She denied it. Vehemently."

"She was trying to keep him out of trouble."

"Yes," Tyrell said, and she felt the bitterness behind the words. "We see that a lot. But until we get something more, Mr. Stouffer isn't a danger to himself or others. Even if he was, we don't have a psychiatric facility here. And even if we did, he doesn't have insurance to pay for it. So if I thought he was truly a safety risk, my only choice would be to call law enforcement and have him locked up. Maybe they'd get him the meds I prescribed, maybe not. The medical care at the county jail is pretty hit or miss. One nurse who contracts her services to three different counties. If she's not there when he gets to the jail, he'll just have to ride out the convulsions. Maybe that's why his wife doesn't want to press this."

"You don't understand," Kate mumbled, but it was hopeless.

What was she going to say? Your patient's under the mental influence of a traveling psychotic who may just be the devil himself?

If she was lucky, the P.A. would laugh in her face. If she wasn't, *she'd* be the one on the way to the nearest locked ward. After all, thanks to COBRA from her former job, she still had the insurance to pay for it.

Tyrell sighed. For a moment, she saw a glimmer of what may have once made him a decent caregiver, and the weight that had squeezed that out of him.

"Take him home," he said. "Let him rest. Give him plenty of water, along with his meds. If his condition worsens, like if he starts convulsing, bring him back, but all we can do then is get him stabilized. I'm sorry."

"Mr. Tyrell, sorry doesn't even begin to cover what you are."

She turned and walked out of the ER and back into the waiting room.

20

IN THE END, IT WAS several hours before Clyde was actually discharged.

Kate wondered if maybe some residual guilt had motivated Tyrell to keep him under observation and medicated as long as possible. Whatever the reason, they made their way back to Clyde and Tara's trailer in darkness.

Tara had followed the ambulance in the couple's one vehicle, and Kate drove Weston and Christopher in her SUV. She pulled up behind Tara's car when they stopped in front of the trailer.

Kate got out at the same time Tara did and met her by the passenger side door where she was helping Clyde out. The young man was pale and drawn, and he leaned against his wife's arm as they started for the front door.

"Let me help you," Kate said as she tried to take up a position on his other side.

"No," Tara told her, her voice polite but firm. "Thank you folks for all your help. I'm taking Clyde in to rest now."

"Tara," Weston said as he walked up, "Let us help you. I can stay here tonight. Just in case he... you know...

takes a bad turn."

Kate could tell the girl was on the ragged edge of exhaustion, but saw her stand up a little straighter, trying to maintain her dignity, and Kate's heart broke as she realized again how young Tara was.

"Thank you," the girl said, as formally as if she was in a receiving line. "Really, I mean that. You've been a real help. But we'll both be fine when we've had some sleep. Y'all drive safe now."

Without another word, she and the silent Clyde made their way across the ragged dirt yard and up to the door of the trailer. As they went inside, Clyde looked back at them.

From where they stood in the outer darkness, they couldn't read his expression, silhouetted as he was against the warm light from inside.

The door swung shut and they were gone.

"Damn it," Weston muttered, and stomped back to the SUV.

Kate joined him, and they climbed in and sat for a long while, watching the trailer.

Nothing happened.

"So what do we do now?" she asked.

Christopher spoke up from the back seat. *I'm hungry.*

"Come to think of it," Weston said, "I could eat."

Kate sighed and nodded. "Considering everything we've been through, I shouldn't be hungry, but I am—and I don't know if there's any food back at the house."

"How about that diner we saw?"

"Is it even open this late?"

"One way to find out."

•

As it turned out, the Singer Cafe was open, if mostly empty. A man in a cook's paper hat and apron left off sweeping behind the long counter and took up his position by the grill.

A plump blond waitress put down the newspaper she'd been reading and slid from her stool, smiling as she approached the booth where they'd taken seats.

"Evenin', folks. Get y'all somethin' to drink?"

"Water for me," Weston said, then pointed at Christopher. "Milk for him."

"Iced tea," Kate said. "Unsweetened."

The waitress frowned. "Unsweet tea?"

From the look on her face, Kate might as well have asked for fermented mare's milk. But she still hadn't gotten used to Southern iced tea, which was typically sweetened to hyperglycemic levels.

"Just water then," she said.

The waitress just nodded and walked away.

Kate rubbed her eyes, which felt raw and gritty from exhaustion. There were a lot of questions roiling in her mind, but she was so addled with fatigue that she couldn't figure out where to begin asking. Finally, she turned to the boy.

"Christopher," she said.

He turned his blind eyes to her. *Yes?*

"I found a notebook. At the trailer."

Lucy's.

Kate was taken aback. "How did you know?"

I just do.

Weston spoke up. "Do you know what was in the book?"

The waitress arrived then, carrying their drinks on a tray. She looked puzzled at the sight of two adults speaking to a blind boy who didn't seem to be answering, but she said nothing as she set them down.

"Ready to order?" She asked brightly as she laid a straw by each glass. "We got one order o' the chicken an' dumplin's left."

"Kate?" Weston said.

"Take it," she answered. "I'll have the club sandwich and fries."

Weston took the chicken and dumplings and ordered a burger for Christopher.

When the waitress was gone, Kate repeated the question. "Do you know what was in the book?"

Drawings. Of me and you and Noah.

"How does she know what we look like?"

The boy just shrugged and Kate looked at Weston. He was frowning.

"Chris," he said, "Is there something you're not telling us?"

I tell you everything I can.

"That's not an answer," Kate said.

The boy didn't respond. He just stirred his milk with his straw.

"Is Lucy like you?" Weston asked. "Does she see things people can't see? Feel things people leave behind?"

"And does she know we're coming?" Kate asked.

Before Chris could answer, the door to the tiny restaurant swung open and a man walked in. Kate recognized Poodie from the garage.

"Hey, Poodie," the waitress called out. "Your order'll be up in a minute."

"Aiiight," Poodie said. He caught sight of the three of them on his way to the counter. "Evenin' folks." He ambled over and stood by the table. "Got that part on order. Should be here tomorrow. At least that's what the trackin' doohickey on the computer says."

"That's great," Weston said. "So we'll be back on the road by afternoon?"

"Yup."

Kate was wishing the man would leave so they could get back to their conversation, but he continued to stand there.

"So how you likin' it over at Father Steve's?" he asked.

"Fine," Weston said.

Poodie nodded. "He's a good guy. I mean for a priest and all. And a, you know..." he trailed off.

Kate stifled a frown. "A Mexican, you mean."

Poodie had apparently missed the tone in her voice. "Yeah. Seen a lot o' them around, you know, but never really got to know any."

Weston had noticed Kate's jaw clenching and he broke in. "Sorta changes the way you look at things, don't it?"

Poodie nodded, looking thoughtful. "I reckon it

does."

The waitress walked up to the table, carrying a brown paper bag. Kate could see the stains where something juicy was dripping through.

She held it out to Poodie. "Here ya go, hon. I snuck in a few extra sweet potato fries for ya."

He took the bag. "Thank you, darlin'," he said with a sly grin. "You're so good to me. Why don't you leave all this, an' let's run away together."

She giggled like a schoolgirl. "Go on with you, now."

He laughed back. "See you later," he said, then turned to Kate and Weston. "Have a good evenin', folks. Sorry again about the delay. Guess this little town's pretty dull for you. We don't offer much here in the way o' nightlife."

Weston smiled. "So far, we're finding plenty to keep us busy."

Poodie scratched his jaw. "Huh. That'd be a first."

He walked away.

As Kate turned back to Christopher, hoping to resume her questioning, the waitress returned.

Damn it, she thought, then she saw and smelled the food and realized just how hungry she was. She spent the next little while eating, her mouth too full to ask questions.

Weston and Christopher also tucked into their meals with a will. The moment they were done, the waitress was back, busily clearing plates and slapping the check down on the table.

"Don't mean to rush you folks, but we're closin' up.

Can I get you some pie? To go?"

"No thanks," Weston said, getting out his wallet as he stood up.

Kate slid out of the booth as well, reaching for her purse.

"I've got this one," he said.

She thought about making an argument of it, but was too tired. "We'll meet you at the car."

Christopher followed her out to the SUV. As they reached it, Kate turned around.

"Look," she said to him, "I don't know what you're hiding, but you're hiding something. This isn't going to work unless we trust each other."

The boy leaned against the passenger side door. He ran his hands through his hair, then folded his arms across his chest and hugged himself tightly. He was clearly agitated about something.

"At least answer me one question," Kate said. "Is he still here? The Beast? Is he here in Singer?"

I don't know, Christopher said. *The river. And* her. *Sometimes it's so loud. In my head.*

Weston came out of the diner and walked up to them. "We ready to get back to the house?"

Kate turned to him. "I think I know why the Beast was here. And why he may still be."

21

"SO," WESTON SAID. "HE'S USING that... whatever it is... in the river as some kind of smokescreen. To hide his trail."

Kate nodded. "Chris keeps saying the river's making so much noise, he's having trouble picking anything up. And I think the Beast knows that. But whether it's him or Lucy who has the gift is anyone's guess. And Chris won't say."

They were sitting on Morales's porch, in the dark. A lone street lamp at the edge of the roadway provided a dim illumination. A cloud of bugs swirled around the light, like animate snowflakes. The high whine of cicadas mingled with the rhythmic chirping of the crickets. From somewhere far away, they could hear a dog barking.

Christopher had gone to bed, falling asleep with the speed only a child could achieve. Shortly after Kate had joined them, Weston had told her that the boy didn't sleep much, but he seemed to be doing a better job of it than her.

"My money's on Lucy," Weston said. "Remember the photo book?"

He was talking about the cheap pink photo album

that Chris once carried with him, even though it had the name *Lucy* scrawled in a childish hand on the cover. Kate had picked it up when she first took Weston in for questioning after finding the two of them at the scene of a murder she'd been investigating. She'd been surprised to open it and discover nothing but the sort of bland, staged generic family photo you'd find in the album if you looked at it in the store.

But on subsequent occasions, she'd picked it up and the album had changed. It seemed to be a window into... she didn't know what. But the pictures were never the same. At one point, while holding it, she'd been mentally transported back to the scene of her own mother's murder. The recollection made her shiver, despite the heat of the Alabama night.

"Of course I remember it," she said.

"You still have it?"

She took a deep breath and nodded, knowing what was coming next. "It's in my luggage. I tried to give it back to Chris, but he told me it was my turn to keep it safe."

"But it's really hers. Lucy's. And it's helped us before."

"And you think that's because of her?" Kate asked. "She's trying to help us?"

"I don't know. But I don't think she's the evil one here."

"You want me to go get it. And look into it."

"I don't see anything when I look at it," Weston said. "It's... I guess it's your version of my sketchpad. It's how Christopher helps you see what he sees."

"He's asleep."

Weston nodded. "Which is why it's a good time to see if maybe it's Lucy who's controlling the thing." He studied her face. "You're scared."

"You're damn right I'm scared. I'm seeing things that make me think that maybe I've gone completely off my rocker and I can't depend on my own sanity." The words seemed to open a floodgate inside of her, and she went on. "I'm in the middle of goddamn nowhere, chasing a maniac who may be some kind of superhuman and who'll cut my tongue out if he catches us. I'm doing things on the word of a psychic little boy who may or may not be telling us the whole truth, but who's also in the line of fire if I screw up. And I don't know if I can depend..." she stopped.

"Go ahead," Weston said quietly. "Say it. You don't know if you can depend on me."

"No. I don't." She'd said more than she wanted to say, but it was out in the open now, and it had to be dealt with, so she stopped his next words with a raised hand. "I know you'll never hurt me. Or Christopher. I trust you completely on that. But if we do catch up with this... this Beast, or if he catches up with us, I don't know that you've really thought through what you'll do next. You won't even carry a gun, and you get all weird when I bring one. How do I know you won't get both of us killed? And that boy sleeping in there?"

Weston got up and walked to the edge of the porch, leaning against one of the pillars that held up the roof. He looked out into the night.

When he spoke, his voice was so low and subdued she could barely hear him. "You're right to be worried. After all, I couldn't protect my wife. Or my little girls."

"That wasn't your fault. There was no way you could have seen that coming." She stood up and went to stand beside him. "And you know why that is? Because you're not like him. You're not a violent man. You've never had to deal with that level of violence before."

"And you have."

"I'm a cop, Noah. Or at least I was. The day I put on the uniform for the first time, I made a commitment that I'd pull the trigger and take another person's life if I had to. But only if I had to. I don't think you've got your head in that place yet."

"Have you ever done it?" he asked. "Pulled the trigger? Taken someone's life?"

"No," she said. "Not yet. I've had a moment where I was sure I was going to, though."

"Did it bother you?"

"Of course. I had the shakes for days. That may have had something to do with the fact that the son of a bitch I nearly killed had a gun pointed at me, but yeah, even getting near to killing someone bothered me. But I put the badge on and went to work the next day. I made the same commitment. Can you?"

It took him a long time to answer.

"Yes," he finally said. "I want him dead. I want the man who murdered my family dead."

"I know you do. But are you willing to kill him? To take a gun, point it at him, and pull the trigger till it clicks empty? Are you willing to take a knife and stab and stab and stab until he stops moving? Are you willing to—"

"I get it!" he flared. "Yes. Yes. And yes. I'll do whatever it takes."

"Good. Now the even bigger question. Are you willing to *not* kill him?"

He shook his head. "Jesus, woman, what the hell is wrong with you?"

"Each of us needs to know where the other stands. I may have turned in my badge, but I still intend to bring this guy in, if I can. I don't get the impression he's gonna want to be taken alive. But that's Plan A. Capture and convict. Kill only if necessary. We on the same page here?"

Weston grimaced. "Can you imagine trying to convict him, on the basis of what we have? A bunch of psychic impressions, a magic photo album, and a boy who can't see or talk?"

"We'll deal with that when the time comes. But are we in agreement here?"

He nodded. "Yeah. I can live with that."

"Okay, then. Tomorrow, we look for a gun for you. Shouldn't be hard to find. This is Alabama, after all. They probably sell them at the 7-Eleven. Then I teach you how to shoot."

He gave her a tired smile. "I grew up in North Carolina. Just because I don't like guns doesn't mean I've never shot one."

"Then I give you a refresher course in how to shoot

correctly. Hope you didn't pick up any bad habits plinking at squirrels or possums on Weston's Ridge or wherever."

"Weston Hill," he said. "And I did all right. But I'm sorry, Kate. Those days are long gone. I'm willing to do whatever needs to be done to stop this maniac, but I won't carry a gun. I already told you why."

"Goddamn it, Noah, how do expect us to—"

"I'm not having this argument with you."

She could see by the look on his face that there was no point in pushing it. Maybe she'd try again later.

If it wasn't too late.

She reached out and gave his arm a squeeze, to let him know things were okay between them. He reached over and placed his hand over hers. They stood there like that for a moment, then he let go. She left her hand in place, then she gave another squeeze and let go.

"Okay," she said. "Now we have a look at the photo album."

22

KATE SAT ON THE FADED couch in the priest's living room, holding the plastic photo album on her lap. Weston sat next to her, close but not touching. Her hand trembled a little as she ran her fingers over the name *Lucy* scrawled on the cover.

She didn't want to open the book. She never knew what to expect. One time it had merely shown her pictures of Lucy as Christopher called to her, across the miles, asking her to join them. But another time, it had taken her to the scene of her mother's murder, all those years ago. And she hadn't been a spectator, but a participant, traveling *inside* Michael Bonner's body.

That wasn't the kind of thing you could easily put behind you.

The album scared her. Christopher scared her. This whole thing terrified her. But she finally opened it anyway.

There was nothing there.

No Lucy, no vision, just the generic family portrait. She felt strangely disappointed as she closed the book.

It doesn't work without me. Or Lucy.

Kate yelped in surprise and dropped the album to the floor. She looked up to see Christopher standing in the doorway. His pale skin and milky white eyes made him look ethereal, like a spirit.

Maybe he is, Kate thought.

"Hey, Chris," Weston said. His voice sounded strained. "You ought to be in bed."

The boy didn't answer. He walked to the couch and sat down between them, squirming until they moved over to give him room.

I guess we need to talk.

"Okay," Kate said.

Weston nodded. "We do have some questions."

You don't know whether to trust me.

The words were said without sadness or anger, just as a bald statement of fact.

"*I* trust you," Weston said.

Kate shot him an angry look. "I just have questions, Chris."

Go ahead and ask.

"Who is Lucy?" Kate said. "Is she your sister?"

Not my sister *sister. But kind of like one.*

"You're close," Weston said, "but not blood kin."

Yes. I told her I'd look after her. But...

The voice in Kate's head trembled. She saw a tear run down the boy's face.

But I didn't. I was too little. I was too weak.

Kate put an arm around his thin shoulders. For all his oddness, he was still just a boy. And that's what she told him.

"You were a just little boy then, Chris. It's not your fault." She gave him a squeeze. "But why did he take her, instead of killing her? Like..." she stopped speaking.

She'd been about to say *like he did you.*

The Beast had actually strangled Chris to death before mutilating him. Somehow, the boy had come back from beyond, and he'd come back changed.

He took her because she's like me. At least sort of.

"She can gather?" Weston asked. "Feel the residue of things that have happened?"

Christopher shook his head. *No. Sometimes she can feel things that are about to happen. Not too far ahead. Just a little bit.*

"A clairvoyant," Kate whispered.

"Handy little partner for a killer to have around," Weston said grimly. "So he does know we're coming."

And she can talk to people. In their heads. The way I do.

"Can the Beast do that, too?"

No. Not exactly. Everyone's different.

"Is he hurting her?" Kate asked.

She thought of the girl's face in the pictures she'd seen in the photo album, shortly before she came to join Chris and Weston. There'd been such a sweetness there, an innocence. Kate's insides twisted at the thought of the little girl being tortured into using her gift to benefit a vicious killer.

No. He's nice to her. That's why she wants to help him.

"Doesn't she know who he is?" Kate said. "What he's done? What he's still doing?"

Not really. She didn't actually see what happened at

the group home. She's beginning to think there's some-thing not right. But... Kate felt a shiver run through the boy's shoulders. *But she still thinks he's a friend. I think he's trying to make her be like him.*

"Dear God," Kate said.

"So you're in touch with her," Weston said.

Yes. He doesn't know that, though. And he doesn't know she's helping us. But she'll do what I ask, because she's my friend.

"Is that why she left the notebook in Tara's house?" Kate said. "To help us?"

I think so. She wants to let you know she's your friend, too.

"Why haven't you told us any of this before?" Weston asked, as gently as he could.

Kate saw another tear run down the boy's face.

I was afraid. I needed to be the only one talking to her. If you knew what she could do... you'd know that you can talk to her, too, like you do me.

"And what's wrong with that?" Kate asked.

Because then you might tell her what the Beast is, what he does. And if she knew that, he could sense it, sense her fear, and hurt her. Even kill her. Or if some-how you let it slip, did something to let him know she's helping us... He was crying openly now, the tears pour-ing down his face. *I didn't want to keep things from you. But I was so afraid...*

Kate wrapped him up in her arms and pulled him to her. He buried his face in her shoulder and cried in deep, racking sobs.

Since the day he had revealed to her what he could do, and the things he'd been through, she had regarded him as something more than an eleven-year-old boy. Somehow immune to the horrors he'd seen. But as she held him now, she knew that she should never lose sight of the fact that he was still a child, trying to cope in a world that had been cruel and unmerciful to him.

"Shhh," she said, running her fingers through his hair. "Shhh..."

After a while, he quieted. He pulled his head away from Kate's shoulder and wiped his nose with the back of his hand.

Weston handed him a bandanna-sized handkerchief out of his pocket. "Gonna have to pick up some more of these," he said with a gentle smile.

Christopher blew his nose. *Thanks.*

He tried to return the handkerchief, but Weston pushed it back into his hand.

"Christopher," he said quietly. "This gift of yours...I know it can be a burden, too. I think sometimes I... we ...forget that."

He looked at Kate and she nodded at the echo of her own thoughts.

"It forces you into decisions a boy your age should never have to make," he went on. "Makes you think about things you shouldn't have to think about. But I want you to know, Chris, that you don't have to bear that burden all on your own shoulders. We're here to help you, as much as you want to help us. You can tell us anything. And if you tell us to back off Lucy, let you be the only one to talk to her, we'll honor that. Okay?"

The boy nodded. *Okay.*

"Can you talk to her now?" Kate asked.

Christopher shook his head. *Sometimes. It's like talking to someone underwater, though. It's all unclear and muffled.*

"Can you tell if she's near? With him?"

Chris wiped his eyes with the bandanna. *No. I can't tell. But maybe. Maybe I wouldn't be able to hear her at all if she wasn't close.*

Kate nodded and rubbed her eyes. She was so tired she felt as if gravity had doubled, then redoubled until the very floor threatened to drag her down.

"You look done in," Weston said. "Maybe we should all get some sleep."

Kate wanted to suggest posting one of them as sentry, but Weston looked as wiped out as she felt.

"Okay," she said. "First we check all the doors and windows."

He nodded. "I'll do that. You turn in."

She did as he asked. But before slipping under the covers, she took her Beretta from her purse and set it on the nightstand.

23

FATHER ESTEBAN MORALES KNELT BEFORE the altar of his church, head bowed. He had been in that position for six hours, and his knees felt like someone had been pounding them with hammers, but he welcomed the pain.

It was far less agony than he deserved.

"O my God," he whispered into the silence, "I am heartily sorry for having offended Thee. I detest all my sins because they offend Thee, my God, Who art all good and deserving of all my love. I firmly resolve, with the help of Thy grace, to confess my sins, to do good, avoid evil, and to amend my life. Amen."

He hadn't put on the robes or the stole; he wasn't worthy to wear them until he could purge this sin from his heart.

The words of St. Matthew's gospel pricked at him like thorns in his flesh:

I say unto you, That whosoever looketh on a woman to lust after her hath committed adultery with her already in his heart.

The only problem was, every time he thought of the words, he saw Tara's face in his mind's eye. He saw her body, slender but strong. He heard her gentle laugh.

I am the rose of Sharon, and the lily of the valleys. As the lily among thorns, so is my love among the daughters.

He wanted nothing more than to hold her in his arms, protect her, tell her everything was going to be all right, and then to make that so.

Was that lust? He didn't know.

He knew it was wrong, though. He was a priest. God had commanded him to put aside the desires of the flesh.

He raised his head to look at the face of the man who hung on the cross before him, seeking some guidance, some sign in that smooth carved visage.

Nothing moved. Nothing spoke. It was just a carving made of wood.

Another verse came into his mind.

My God, my God, why hast thou forsaken me? Why art thou so far from helping me, and from the words of my roaring?

He spoke the next verse aloud. "O my God, I cry in the day time, but thou hearest not; and in the night season, and am not silent."

Nothing answered.

Morales rubbed his tired eyes. Slowly, he got to his feet. He needed sleep. He needed food. Maybe tomorrow...

His thoughts were interrupted by a familiar sound: The front door of the church opening with a long, drawn out creak.

Morales frowned. He couldn't see who was entering.

The front door opened onto a small vestibule, and the door from the sanctuary to the vestibule was closed.

"Hello?" he called out. "Who's there?"

He doubted that it was one of his parishioners, come to make a late night confession. They were an older congregation who tended to go to bed early. He wondered if some drunk or homeless person had wandered in, seeking shelter or a place to sleep.

The door to the vestibule didn't open. He sighed and walked down the aisle toward the closed door.

"I'm sorry," he said as he pulled it open, "we're closed for the—"

He stopped and stared in puzzlement. There was no one there. The outside door was just closing.

Now he was irritated. He strode across the vestibule and pushed the door open. The moist heat of the night billowed in. But there was still no one there.

He stepped out onto the front steps of the church and looked around. He couldn't see anyone on the short lawn between the steps and the sidewalk, or the sidewalk itself.

He looked across the street at his house.

What he saw there made him blink in shock.

Then he broke into a run, headed toward home.

•

Despite her weariness and the comfort of the big bed, sleep was slow in coming to Kate, and when it did come, it was an uneasy slumber, broken by sudden shocks of wakefulness that made her gasp and sit bolt upright, groping for her weapon on the bedside table.

Finally, exhaustion triumphed and she fell into a deep sleep. Even then, however, she was troubled by dreams of dark figures moving in the fog beside an ancient and sluggish river, its black water roiled by leviathans in the depths, silky whispers she couldn't quite make out because of the wind that blew steadily, remorselessly, across the face of the water.

She strained to hear the words, despite the certainty that there was evil there that could drive her to madness and reduce her soul to a shriveled husk. From time to time, she could hear a sound that made no sense in that Stygian dreamscape: the sound of a child laughing.

A little girl.

Kate opened her eyes. She turned and squinted at the clock on the bedside table. 4:38.

There was something wrong with the light in her room. The overhead was off, as was the bedside lamp, but the room seemed strangely bright, with a light that flickered and danced oddly...

She came fully awake and rolled over, looking toward the window. The light was coming from there, a bright orange flare like a rising sun improbably ascending just outside.

Something was on fire.

"NOAH!" she shouted, throwing the covers off and swinging her legs out of the bed.

She grabbed up her jeans off the floor and pulled them on. From the next room, she heard the thump of

Weston's feet hitting the floor.

She was pulling her T-shirt on over her head as she nearly collided with him coming out of the bedroom. He beat her to the front door by a half-second and yanked it open. She followed him out onto the front porch, where she saw where the light was coming from.

Her SUV was on fire.

Bright orange flames billowed from the interior and from under the hood. The stink of burning plastic and hot metal filled the air.

Kate stood there, stunned into immobility for a moment. She saw a flash of movement and turned to see Father Morales running across the street from the church.

"Father!" Weston shouted. "We need a hose!"

Morales stopped at the curb and stared wide eyed at the flaming vehicle.

"MORALES!" Weston shouted.

The priest turned to him, his face blank with shock.

"A HOSE!"

When Morales didn't respond, Weston swore under his breath. He turned to Kate.

"Go inside," he said. "Call 911. I'll try to find some water. We've got to get this area wetted down before the trees and the house catch."

Kate nodded. Calling backup was something she could instinctively understand.

She dashed back into the house and nearly crashed into Christopher. The boy was standing in the living room, his head cocked slightly in that familiar listening pose.

He was smiling.

Kate, he said in her mind. *I hear her. I hear Lucy.*

"That's great, Chris, but we've got a problem."

She pushed past him into the kitchen, where she located the phone on the wall. She grabbed it and dialed 911.

A female voice came on the line. "911, what's the nature of your—"

Kate interrupted her, her police training taking over.

"Dispatch," she barked, "We've got an 11-71 at..." she trailed off, realizing that she didn't know any of the street addresses here. "Across from St. Michael's. In Singer."

"A what?" The voice on the other end sharpened with suspicion. "Who is this?"

"Goddamn it," Kate muttered. Of course the police codes in this backwater were different from the ones where she'd made her career.

The voice turned icy. "Ma'am, there's no need to use that kind of—"

"There's a fire!" she shouted. "In Singer! I don't know the address! It's across from the Catholic church!"

That got through. "Okay, ma'am," the voice said, suddenly brisk and professional. "I've got your location from the system. Don't hang up. Is anyone injured?"

"No. Not yet. A couple of people are trying to contain the fire."

She looked through the kitchen door. She saw

Christopher, still standing in the living room. All at once, she realized the implications of what he'd said.

I hear Lucy.

Which might mean Lucy was near. And if she was near...

"Dispatch," Kate said in a low, urgent voice, "we're going to need law enforcement here. This looks like arson. And the subject or subjects may still be in the area."

There was a brief pause. "Ma'am, you sound like you might be in law enforcement yourself."

"Used to be," Kate said. "And dispatch, there may be something seriously hinky going on here. Tell your officers to be careful."

"Copy that," the voice said. Then, "Oh. I need to get your name."

"Kate Messenger."

"Thanks, Kate. Now, think you can be more specific about what my boys need to be careful about?"

"If the guy who burned my vehicle is who I think it is, he ought to be considered armed and extremely dangerous. That's all I can say right now."

"I need more information than that," the dispatcher said.

For the second time in twenty-four hours, Kate could hear the sound of sirens in the distance.

"I just wish I had more to give," she said, then she hung up the phone.

The sirens were getting closer. She went out into the living room. Christopher was still standing there, like a statue.

"Christopher," she said softly.

He turned his blind eyes toward her. *Yes, Kate?*

She put a hand on his shoulder. "Is he here? The Beast?" She gestured toward the open door, where she could still see the reflections of the flames dancing. "Did he do this?"

Instead of answering, Christopher walked to the front door. Kate's hand fell from his shoulder as she followed him.

He stopped in the doorway and she pulled up short behind him. She could see the fire trucks coming, their red and white and yellow lights pulsing in the darkness.

Morales was pulling a green garden hose around from the side yard, but it looked as if it wouldn't be needed.

As the first truck, a yellow and silver pumper, pulled up, Christopher began that strange back and forth rocking motion, and that told Kate all she needed to know.

They're near, he said.

At that moment, she heard the sound of gunfire.

24

WESTON WAS TURNING THE HANDLE on the outside spigot when he heard the first shots ring out. First one, then three in quick succession, then it sounded as if a battery of rifles was opening up.

Christopher, he thought.

Kate.

He bolted toward the front of the house, heedless of the sound of the gunfire. He nearly collided with Morales, who was standing there dumbly, the useless hose in his hand.

"Get down!" Weston shouted.

Another sharp report, and the windshield of the SUV blew out. Something whined through the air, a few inches from Weston's shoulder.

He decided to take his own advice. He grabbed the priest's shirt and dropped to the ground, pulling Morales with him.

Another bullet whizzed by over their heads.

"It's coming from inside the car!" Morales said.

Damn it, Weston thought. Did that fool woman leave her gun in the car?

He could see the firefighters scattering at the sound of the shots. A police cruiser pulled up, siren wailing. A pair of blue-clad patrolmen piled out of the car, drawing their sidearms as they took cover behind their vehicle.

"Christopher!" Weston shouted.

The boy's voice filled his head.

We're okay, Noah.

The fusillade of explosions was slowing, like the last few kernels of popcorn popping in the microwave.

Morales started to get up, but Weston pulled him back down again. "Stay down. Those cops are liable to shoot anyone they can see."

The car was still burning brightly. There was a sudden whoosh and a bigger ball of flame erupted from the burning vehicle as the gas tank ruptured and the remaining fuel ignited.

Weston felt the rush of heated air wash over him and saw the bushes near the front door beginning to shrivel and smoke. The trees near the driveway were starting to catch.

"We better move back," he told Morales. He started to belly-crawl in reverse away from the burning vehicle and the front of the house.

"POLICE!" a voice shouted from behind them. "DON'T MOVE!"

"HANDS WHERE I CAN SEE THEM!" another voice shouted.

Damn it, Weston thought.

Slowly, he pushed his hands out in front of him, spreading his fingers wide to show they were empty.

"I'm unarmed," he called out.

He felt the pressure of a knee on his back, digging into his spine. The person behind him leaned more weight on him, making him groan with the pain. "I *said* I'm unarmed."

"Shut up, asshole." The voice had a thick country accent.

Weston felt something pressed against the back of his neck. "Hands behind your back."

The pressure let up as he complied. He felt the cold embrace of handcuffs being fastened around his wrists. As he was yanked to his feet, he saw Morales undergoing the same treatment a few feet away.

Firefighters were approaching the burning SUV, hoses spewing white foam.

A hand on Weston's shoulder turned him to face a short, broad cop with red hair and freckles. He had lost his hat, and his shock of red hair was mussed, standing up on his head in places. He looked about fifteen years old.

"Where's the gun?" he demanded. Weston could see the whites of his eyes. The kid was scared to death.

"Easy, son." He kept as low and calm a voice as he could muster. "I don't have a gun. Never did."

He nodded to where another cop, this one a gangly, raw-boned beanpole of a man who didn't look much older than the redhead, was shouting at Morales.

"And that guy's the priest at St. Michael's. He lives in this house."

The redhead looked in confusion from Weston, to Morales, then back to Weston. He was panting like a racehorse.

Weston went on, trying his best to still the young cop from panicking and doing something stupid. "The gun was in the car. What you heard was the ammunition cooking off." He frowned as he recalled the number of explosions he'd heard. "A lot of ammunition."

It must have been at least a box's worth. He didn't remember Kate having a box of spare ammo, just the gun in her purse. And he'd seen the purse in the house, before they went to bed.

He began to realize what was happening. All the pieces were arranging themselves in his mind.

"Son of a bitch..." he murmured.

The redheaded cop bristled. Resistance was something he could understand, and knew how to deal with. "What'd you say to me, asshole?"

Weston shook his head. "Nothing, son. Nothing at all."

And he hoped he was wrong about this, but knew within a hair's breadth of certainty that he wasn't.

They had just been played.

•

An hour later, dawn was breaking outside.

The three of them sat on the couch in a line. Weston, Kate, and Morales. Christopher was in the other room with a sheriff's deputy and a plump, tired looking woman from Social Services.

The sheriff's detective who had come down from the county seat to take over the scene from the local cops had dragged a chair in from the dining room and sat in front of the couch. He'd taken his suit jacket off and hung it on the back of the chair. He was a genial, round faced man with thinning gray hair. His name was Paulson and he smiled a lot.

Weston didn't hold much trust for police officers, but he was particularly leery of ones who smiled a lot.

Paulson said, "Sorry about the handcuffs, gentlemen. But with a report of shots fired, and," he nodded in Kate's direction, "a report of a potentially armed and dangerous subject in the area, well, we just naturally couldn't take any chances. I figure y'all understand."

"I understand," Morales said, but from his stiff posture, it was clear he was angry.

Paulson smiled. "*Gracias*, padre."

Weston saw the priest's jaw clench at the condescending tone, and he found himself liking Mr. Law and Order even less.

Paulson turned to Kate. "Now, Miss, Messenger, is it?" Kate nodded. It was clear she didn't like Paulson much either. "So, it was your vehicle, correct?"

"Yes, detective, that's right."

Paulson smiled even wider. "Now, we don't need to be all formal, considerin' you were once in law enforcement yourself. You can call me Charlie."

She gave him back a tight, professional smile. "Okay, Charlie. It was my car."

"So, Kate, you got anybody mad enough at you to set it on fire?"

Weston glanced at her.

She shook her head. "No. No, I don't."

Weston hoped he was keeping the surprise off his face. If, as Christopher said, Lucy and the Beast were nearby, it was likely that *he* had set the fire, to hinder their pursuit. That could only mean he was on the move again, like a fox breaking cover and bolting away.

And the hounds were all tied up.

But why would Kate keep that to herself now, after telling Morales all about it?

Paulson turned to the priest. "How about you, Father? Anyone mad at you?"

Morales hesitated. Paulson leaned forward slightly, his eyes bright.

Finally Morales shook his head. "No. No one."

"You sure about that?"

"Of course I am."

"Oh?" Paulson said. "What about Clyde Stouffer?"

25

MORALES'S EYES NARROWED. "WHAT ABOUT him?"

Paulson leaned back, too casually.

Kate tried not to grit her teeth. This guy was such an amateur. And they didn't have time for this. Christopher had let her know what he'd heard when Lucy finally broke her silence.

They've been down by the river, he'd told her. *Camping. She thought it was cool. But it's why I couldn't hear her. But now they're moving. They're getting away, Kate. We need to stop them.*

Paulson was smiling again. "Word in town is that Clyde thinks maybe you and his pretty lil' wife have a thing goin' on. He ain't shy about tellin' people what he means to do about it neither."

Kate had to break in. "So your theory is that Clyde Stouffer torched *my* car because he's mad at *Father Morales*? This makes sense to you?"

Paulson spread his hands in a "who knows?" gesture.

"I don't have any theory at all, Kate. I'm just tryin' to get all the facts here. And one fact I know is that Clyde Stouffer's a mean drunk. Could be he mistook your car for the padre's here."

"That's ridiculous. Clyde knows my car. We just took

him home from the hospital. And, by the way, he was as weak as a kitten when his wife got him in the door. He couldn't have lit a candle in his condition, much less torched my car."

Paulson frowned. "The hospital? What for?"

"He tried to drink himself to death. Then he tried to drown himself."

Kate was getting impatient. She could almost hear the clock ticking, each second taking their quarry farther and farther away. But she had no intention of letting this clown join in the chase. He'd most likely trip over his own feet.

Huh, she thought.

She was starting to think like Noah.

She stood up. "Look, Detective... I mean, Charlie... it's been a long night. I need to get a cup of coffee and call my insurance company..." She stopped talking because she could see that Paulson had stopped listening.

The redheaded patrolman had entered the room from outside and was whispering in his ear. Paulson nodded and turned to Kate with a bland expression on his face that made her guts twist with apprehension.

"I think you better sit down, Kate."

"I'll stand, if you don't mind."

Weston stood up as well.

"Suit yourself." Paulson got to his feet. "That gun in the car? The one with all the ammunition cooking off? Funny thing. The box of ammo was out on the seat. But the gun itself was in a metal lockbox. Unloaded. It was damaged, but we could still get the serial numbers off it."

Kate realized with a sickening feeling of dread what was coming next.

"Turns out that firearm was stolen during a home invasion in South Carolina a couple of weeks ago." He motioned to the redheaded patrolman, who took the handcuffs off his belt. "I think y'all better come with us."

•

Clyde Stouffer woke up, dry mouthed and shivering. The bedsheets were damp and clammy. He'd been sweating like crazy.

He rolled over and fumbled for the bottle of Ativan on the bedside table. His hands were trembling so badly he nearly dropped the bottle onto the floor. After a couple of fumbling attempts, he gave up.

"Tara?" he called out. His voice was a dry croak. He got a little more volume out of the next try.

She appeared in the doorway.

"Hey," she said in a soft voice.

He couldn't read the expression on her face, but she still looked and sounded like an angel to him. He wondered how he could ever have thought she'd do him wrong or how he'd ever dreamed of hurting her.

I'm gonna get better, he told himself. I'm gonna be better.

The thought made him feel a little stronger. "I can't get this bottle open, sugar. An' I could use some water to wash this pill down with."

She nodded. "I figured you'd be thirsty."

She came the rest of the way into the room and he could see she was carrying a bottled water. She sat down on the bed next to him and twisted the top off before handing it over.

He tipped it up, swallowing quickly. It brought back a sense memory, the feeling of tipping up a pint of Jack, the recollection of the liquor burning its way down his throat...

With a gasp, he brought the now half empty bottle down. Tara was holding out her hand. A pair of tiny white tablets rested in the palm.

He fumbled them out of her hand, nearly dropping them before managing to get them into his mouth. When he'd washed them down with the rest of the water, he closed his eyes and leaned against her, putting his head on her shoulder.

"I'm sorry, angel girl," he whispered. "I am so *fucking* sorry."

"Shhhh," she said, running her fingers through his hair. "It's okay."

He realized how long and greasy his hair had gotten.

And I probably stink too, he thought with a flash of shame.

She didn't seem to mind. He never wanted it to end, but after a few minutes, she pulled gently away. "I got to go to work, baby."

He felt a brief stab of the old jealousy, the dark rage, but pushed them both away from him in his mind.

No. She's good. She loves me. Not him. Not that... the savage, hurting words wanted to bubble up inside his mind again, but he wouldn't let them.

She went on. "There's soup in the cupboard. And saltines. You need to eat somethin', okay? And drink plenty of water. The doctor said not to let you get too dehydrated."

He nodded. "Okay."

She walked to the door and turned back. "You rest now. Call me if you need anything."

As she left, he fell back onto the sweat soaked bed. He could feel the shakes starting again. The thought of even trying to sip a little chicken soup made him want to retch.

He'd never felt this awful in his life, even that time when he'd gotten food poisoning from a hot dog at the football game. What made it even worse was that he knew exactly what would make this bad feeling go away.

Just one drink, he thought. Not even a whole drink. One shot's all I need to level me out.

He heard their car start up, heard Tara pulling away.

He ran out of the bedroom, headed toward the front door. He wanted to yank it open, tell her to come back, to take him to town. He just needed one drink...

He was halfway there when he stopped, bent over, hands on knees, panting like he'd just run the hundred yard dash.

Okay. Get a hold of yourself. She's gone. There's no liquor. You can do this.

He straightened up. A shower. He'd feel better after a shower.

Once in the bathroom, however, he thought about the pint of Jack he'd hidden in the cabinet under the sink.

Just need to check and see if it's there. I'll pour it out. I swear.

But when he looked, it was gone.

She must have taken it, the little... He pushed the words away again. Moving like an old man, he undressed and got in the shower.

If he'd hoped it would make him feel better, he was wrong. He'd never imagined that water hitting his body could actually hurt. Everything hurt. He wondered if anything would ever feel good again.

After a few minutes, he'd had all he could stand. He staggered out of the shower and back into the bedroom. He sat naked on the bed for a long time, staring off into space, hurting. Then he fell backward onto the sheets, now wet again, and fell into a twitchy, haunted sleep.

A pounding on the door woke him up.

"What the fuck," he groaned as he tried to sit up. He almost fell over onto the floor.

The pounding continued.

Swearing under his breath, Clyde pulled on a pair of jeans and staggered, shirtless and barefoot, to the front door.

As he yanked it open, he snarled, "What the hell do you—"

He stopped himself at the sight of the grinning man in the doorway.

Marshall Beaumont.

"Hey," Clyde said. "I thought you left town."

Beaumont kept grinning. "Actually, I'm on my way right now."

He held up a bottle.

Clyde's eyes zeroed in on the dark, rich brown liquid inside. He licked his lips.

"I thought we might have a last drink before I left," Beaumont said. "And talk about what Little Miss Hot Pants Tara is getting up to right about now."

26

"THE ONLY PROBLEM WITH YOUR theory, *Charlie*," Kate bit down hard on the last word, "is that two weeks ago, we were nowhere near South Carolina. We were in St. Louis, Missouri."

"You got any way of proving that?" Paulson asked.

"Last I heard," Weston said in a low, angry voice, "we're not the ones who have to prove anything."

"Save me the lawyer bullshit." All of the false friendliness of Paulson's earlier tone was gone. "And both of you put your hands behind your backs. You're both under arrest for possession of a stolen firearm."

Kate frowned. "Think for just a minute, Detective. If we really did have a stolen gun in the car, do you think I'd leave it on the front seat? In a box, so it'd just happen to survive a fire that brought you here? Doesn't that just seem a little too convenient?"

"You have to admit," Morales began.

"Shut up, Father," Paulson snapped. "And I'm not telling you two again. Turn around and put your hands behind your backs."

"What about Clyde Stouffer?" Morales demanded. "Have you forgotten the reason you came here in the first place?"

That stopped Paulson for a moment.

He turned to the redheaded cop. "Jesse, help me get these two in the car. Then get out to Stouffer's residence. See if he can account for where he's been the last 24 hours. And check the hospital. See if he was actually there." He turned back to Kate and Weston. "Now, are you two coming with me, or are we going to make an argument of it that you're bound to lose?"

Kate looked him in the eyes for a long moment. Then she turned her back, facing the couch, and put her hands behind her.

Reluctantly, Weston did the same.

"Father," he said as the redheaded cop cuffed him, "as soon as Poodie's opens, get over there. Look in the glove compartment of my car. The Rambler. There're receipts in there for the places we've been. Motels. Gas stations. Take them to the police station so we can show these idiots," he winced as the redheaded cop tightened the cuffs just a little too much as retaliation for the insult, "where we've been."

"I will. What about Christopher?"

Paulson raised his voice and called toward the other room. "Becky?"

The social worker came out. She was a middle-aged woman with frizzy blond hair, a gap between her front teeth, and bags under her eyes that didn't just come from being called out of bed early.

She shrugged. "It's a little difficult to figure out what's going on because the boy can't talk."

"He has a name," Weston said. "It's Christopher."

The woman ignored him. "When I say he can't talk, I mean he physically can't. His tongue's been amputated."

Paulson sucked in his breath. The woman raised a hand to stop his next words. "He insists that neither of these two people had anything to do with that."

The redheaded cop had gone pale. "How can he tell you that with no tongue?"

The social worker looked at him wearily. "He can hear, Jesse. He can nod his head for yes and shake it for no."

The cop looked embarrassed. "Oh. Right."

For the first time, the social worker noticed that Kate and Weston were in handcuffs. "What's going on here?"

"Taking them in," Paulson said. "Possession of a stolen firearm."

"Ah," the woman said. "Before you do that, let me ask them who the boy's legal guardian is."

Weston turned to face her. "That would be me."

She looked at him up and down, with an expression on her face that indicated she was less than impressed by what she saw. "Right. Are you a parent?"

He shook his head. "No."

"Do you have a court order granting you guardianship?"

Kate could see where this was going. She broke in. "It was in my car."

"Uh-huh," the social worker said. "And where was the original order entered so we can get a copy?"

Kate held her breath, hoping Weston had picked up

on the lie and why it needed to be told.

He had.

"New Orleans," he said.

The woman sighed. "And I suppose this would have been conveniently right before Hurricane Katrina?"

He smiled tightly at her. "Afraid so."

Her return smile was equally insincere. "Well, that means only one thing to do. Until we can get something in writing, we don't have any choice but to assume that Christopher's a dependent child. That means he's without a parent, legal guardian, or legal custodian willing and able to provide for the care, support, or education of the child." She rattled off the last part as if she was quoting from a book.

"But Noah's been doing all of that," Kate protested.

"Not under any legal right," the social worker said. "Without a court order or power of attorney from the parents, he can't enroll the child in..." She stopped. "How long has it been since Christopher was in school?"

"It's summer," Weston replied.

"And before that?"

Weston hesitated. That was all the social worker needed.

"That's what I thought," she said. "Educational neglect." She nodded at Paulson. "Okay, I'm done."

"Let's go," Paulson told Kate and Weston.

"Wait!" Weston said, sounding desperate. "Where are you taking Christopher?"

"Foster care," the social worker said. "And no, I'm not

telling you where."

Kate could sense that Weston was getting close to exploding. Then she heard Christopher's voice in her head.

Don't worry. We'll find each other.

How? Kate thought, hoping the question had somehow gotten through to him.

But he was silent as they led her and Weston to the detective's car.

27

IN HIS FIVE YEARS AS the youngest officer on Singer's three-man police department, Jesse Ottway had had plenty of opportunities to deal with Clyde Stouffer. He wondered if today would be the day they finally threw down.

Stouffer had been getting in Jesse's face, going right up to the line where Jesse would have to cuff his drunk ass and haul him in, but never crossing it.

The last time they'd crossed paths, in the parking lot of Grace's Tavern out on the highway, Stouffer had called him a "redheaded Opie-lookin' motherfucker."

That one still rankled, especially since it had gotten a big laugh from the other drunks milling around after closing time. That crowd, and the fact that a couple of Stouffer's buddies had hustled him away, is why Jesse hadn't busted the little peckerwood's teeth in with his baton.

But today, it would be just the two of them. Jesse smiled a little at that. He'd been scared half to death by all the explosions back at the car fire, thinking someone was shooting at him. It was embarrassing to find out it was just loose ammo cooking off inside the car.

He looked forward to getting some of his swagger

back, and there was no better way to do that than by putting some punk in his place.

As he drove up the overgrown driveway, however, Jesse spotted a vehicle he didn't recognize, an old Ford F-150 pickup with the crew cab. He frowned as he braked to a stop.

"Dispatch," he said into his radio, "Unit 55 is 10-23 at 1534 Old River Road."

"10-4," the answer came back.

As he got out, he slid his baton into the holder on his belt.

"Clyde?" he called out. "Hey, Clyde?"

Before approaching the front door, he walked around the pickup. He noted a couple of stuffed toys in the back of the crew cab. Some raggedy ass doll and a penguin.

Not Clyde and Tara's truck, then—unless they had a kid nobody knew about.

Jesse mounted the rickety wooden steps to the front door and banged on it with his fist.

"Singer PD," he called out. "Open up, Clyde."

The reply came back muffled by the metal door. "It's open."

Jesse hesitated a moment before turning the knob and pulling on it.

Clyde was sitting on the couch in the trailer's living room. There was a three-quarter empty bottle of Jack Daniel's on the beat-up coffee table in front of him. A cigarette dangled from one corner of his mouth. His eyes were so bloodshot they practically glowed red.

"Howdy, Opie," he drawled.

Jesse's jaw tightened and he stepped just inside the doorway. That was when he saw the blood on Clyde's arms and hands.

His hand dropped to his belt and he unsnapped his holster.

Clyde picked up something from the table. Jesse saw a glint of metal in the light from the open door.

Knife.

He put his hand on the butt of his sidearm. "Easy, Clyde," he said. "Put the knife down."

Clyde didn't move. "Jus' a second," he mumbled. "Almos' done." He brought the tip of the knife to the inside of his wrist and began working it into the flesh.

Jesse was shocked into immobility for a second. He recovered quickly and drew his weapon.

"Put the knife *down*," he said, hating the way his voice trembled.

Clyde looked up and smiled the worst smile Jesse had ever seen. There was no pleasure or humor in it, only an insane malevolence.

He dropped the knife to the floor and held up both hands, the inside of his wrists facing Jesse. Through the blood streaming down and dripping onto the threadbare carpet, Jesse could see what Clyde had been doing.

Carved into the flesh of each wrist was a ragged circle. He'd made a smaller puncture wound in the center of the circle.

"Hands up," Clyde said, and giggled. "Don't shoot."

Jesse involuntarily took a step back. He *felt* rather than heard someone or something on the stairs behind him, but the sight of Clyde's act of self-mutilation had so unnerved him that it took him a half second too long to respond.

He felt a huge hand grab the collar of his uniform shirt and yank him backward off the steps. He stumbled, lost his balance, and went crashing to the ground. His gun flew from his hand.

He lay there for a moment, stunned, the wind knocked out of him, then something came between him and the sun.

Something dark.

He heard a sound—an eerie whistle—slashing through the air, then his belly seemed to explode with pain. He looked down in horror to see an ax embedded in his stomach.

He was too stunned to scream until the man standing above him yanked the ax free, the blade dripping with blood and bits of tissue that Jesse realized were from inside him.

He shrieked then, a high inhuman howl of agony and despair.

The ax whistled again and the scream was cut off as the heavy sharpened metal head smashed through his sternum and into the center of his chest.

There was nothing left in Jesse's universe but pain, so much agony that he welcomed the blackness he felt rushing up to envelop him.

Anything to make it stop.

As his vision began to fade, Jesse saw the figure stoop down beside him. He sobbed as another blade glinted, this one coming at his face.

He felt something grab his jaw and pull his mouth open.

No, he wanted to say, *don't*, but the words wouldn't come.

He felt a hot breath in his ear, then a voice so harsh and evil it felt as if it was rolling out of the pits of Hell itself whispered in his ear. "The mouth of the just bringeth forth wisdom," it said, "but the froward tongue shall be cut out."

Mercifully, Jesse died before the cutting began.

28

"THANKS, TED," FATHER MORALES SAID into the phone. "I owe you one."

He hung up and sighed. He didn't like asking personal favors from parishioners. He knew it could be a slippery slope from there to the kind of abuse of power that could lead to resentments and defection from the Church.

But Kate and Weston needed a lawyer, and Teodoro "Ted" Garcia was not only one of the area's best-connected, he was the only one Morales knew. Garcia had promised to get by the jail as soon as calendar call in district court was done.

Morales rubbed his tired eyes. What he really wanted was sleep. He hadn't had much of that the past couple of days.

He looked at the clock on the wall. A little after 8:30. Poodie's garage would just be opening, and he needed to get there. Weston had said there were documents in the car's glove box that would prove they couldn't have stolen that gun.

Promises to keep, he thought. Miles to go before I sleep.

•

Clyde looked down at the dead police officer. Something in the back of his mind told him he should be more worried about this, more freaked out by the gaping, bloody holes in the young man's body or the blood all around his mouth.

That voice, however, was faint and far away. It was no match for the other voice, the one of the man who stood beside him.

Still, a glimmer of sense remained.

"Shouldn't we bury him?" he said to Beaumont.

"No," Beaumont said. "He's meat. Leave him for the crows." He bent down to the cop's leg and started pulling a shoe off. "Here," he said, "help me."

Clyde obeyed. In a few minutes they had the dead cop's uniform off.

Beaumont held it out to him. "Put it on."

Clyde and the dead man were about the same height, but the cop had been working out and was much stockier where Clyde was rail thin and wiry. Clyde had to cinch the shiny leather belt to its last notch, and even then, he kept hitching at the waistband to keep the pants from sliding down from the weight of the holster, cuffs, and other gear clipped to it. The uniform shirt hung on him like a hand-me-down.

When Beaumont put the hat on Clyde's head, it slid down over his eyes.

"Perfect," Beaumont said.

"Perfect," Clyde echoed, then another coherent question bubbled up out of the depths of his disordered mind. "Hey. Where's that lil' girl of yours?"

"At our camp, by the river. When we get done here, I'm gonna go pick her up, and then we're on our way."

"By the river? All by herself?" Clyde shook his head as if to clear the cobwebs, but the cobwebs stayed put. "Ain't you worried?"

Beaumont laughed, a low, rumbling chuckle that made Clyde feel uneasy.

"Lucy's fine," he said. "She's playing with her new friend. You know who I mean."

Clyde shuddered. He remembered the time he and Beaumont were down by the waterside, and the shadow that moved just below the water. He'd heard that shadow singing to him. The song had drawn him toward the river, but Beaumont always stopped him.

But he left his little girl down there, and her bein' retarded and all...

"Don't worry," Beaumont assured him, as if he'd read his mind. "*She* won't hurt a girl. Or a woman. They never did her any harm. Which is why you don't give her Tara. You give her the boy. You hear that? Give her the blind boy. *She*'s very interested in him. Then the priest. But Tara? She's all yours, partner."

"All mine," Clyde repeated. He shook his head. "No. Wait. I don't want to—"

Beaumont reached out and put his hand on Clyde's head. Suddenly, his brain became a kaleidoscope of images, all of them obscene, as if every porno he'd ever seen on his computer or DVD player was playing at once. And all of them starred Tara and the priest:

Tara riding him, moving slow, her eyes closed, her

mouth gaping in pleasure, Tara on her hands and knees with Morales behind her, her eyes glazed with ecstasy, Tara trailing her tongue across his muscular chest, circling his nipples, her eyes full of laughter as she moved that tongue lower... lower... and that laughter was directed at him, at Clyde, at her stupid drunken husband...

"The mouth of the just bringeth forth wisdom," he heard Beaumont say.

Clyde finished the quote: "but the froward tongue shall be cut out."

Beaumont clapped him on the shoulder. "It's been a real pleasure knowing you, partner. I'm just sorry I won't be around to watch all the fun. But I've gotta be moving on." He smiled. "Now go do what you've gotta do."

29

"SORRY, FATHER," POODIE SAID, "I CAN'T just let you go rummagin' around in a customer's car. Not without his permission."

"But you don't understand," Morales told him. "Kate and Noah have been arrested. They're accused of something they didn't do."

"Arrested?" Griff said from the doorway between the garage and the office. "Dang."

Poodie turned to him, scowling. "Ain't there enough work for you to do?"

"That's what I was gonna tell you. The water pump for that Rambler just come in. You want me to put it in?"

Poodie got up from his chair, shifting his bulk with difficulty. "Hell no. You don't know nothin' about those classic cars."

Griff looked wounded. "Well, how different can it be?"

"I said, I'd do it."

Griff had to step out of the way as Poodie pushed past him into the garage.

Griff sighed and shook his head. "I don't care if he is family, this shit's gettin' old." He looked at the priest.

"One o' these days, man, I'm gonna go work for some-one who don't treat me like shit."

"Griff," Morales said, "can you do me a favor?"

"Look in the glove box and see what I can find?" Griff shook his head. "Nuh-uh. Poodie'd shit-can me in a hot second, family or not."

Morales's heart sank until Griff went on.

"Tell you what I will do, though. Soon as we get that baby runnin' I'll deliver her personally up to the county jail, and, well, if somethin' happens to fall out of the glove box on the way, ain't nothin' I can do about that, now is there? And if it does, an' it looks like it might be helpful, well, I jus' can't help but do my civic duty an' take it to someone, right?"

"Ted Garcia," Morales said. "He's agreed to be their lawyer."

Griff nodded. "Yeah, I hear he's a good 'un."

"He is. You think Poodie'll let you take the Rambler up to the jail?"

Griff rubbed his chin. "Huh. That could be a problem. He don't usually let a car leave the garage unless it's paid for."

"Then I guess I'll have to do something about that."

Morales reached into his back pocket and pulled out his checkbook. Griff's eyes widened in surprise.

"Dang," he said. "You're gonna pay their bill?"

"They'll pay me back," Morales told him. "I have faith. Let me borrow your pen."

•

After leaving a signed blank check with Griff, Morales

headed back home.

He'd done what he could do for Kate and Weston and now it was time to get some sleep.

But when he arrived at the house he saw Tara's car parked in the driveway. The burned out hulk of Kate's SUV was gone, towed away by the sheriff's deputies for further analysis.

He pulled to a stop by the curb. He didn't get out of the car.

He hadn't thought she'd come to work today, and the familiar turmoil of emotions rolled and tumbled inside his mind again.

He didn't want to see her.

He wanted to see her more than he'd ever wanted anything.

It was a terrible idea for him to get anywhere near her, feeling the way he did right now.

It was an idea he couldn't let go of.

He ran his hands through his hair and closed his eyes. When he opened them again, he saw her standing on the front porch, watching him.

He got out of the car and walked slowly toward her. She didn't move or speak, just watched him approach.

When he reached the porch, he stopped, looking up at her.

"Hey," she said softly.

"Hey," he replied.

"You gonna come in?"

He suddenly felt as awkward as a teenager on his first date. "I guess I should."

She laughed. "Well, it *is* your house."

He knew he should ask how Clyde was doing. Before he could, she turned and walked back inside.

He followed her. As he entered the darkened house, she was standing there, looking at him. As he closed the door, she came closer, her gaze never wavering.

Then she was in his arms. He wrapped them around her and pulled her against him, closing his eyes. Her body felt so warm and soft next to his, and the clean scent of her hair made him want to bury his face in it.

"I..."

"Hush," she whispered. "Just hold me, okay? That's all I want. I promise. I just need you to hold me."

"Okay," he said hoarsely.

His head felt as if it was about to explode.

Your vows, part of his mind was raging. What about your vows?

Another part of that same mind could only marvel at the way they seemed to fit together perfectly. That part never wanted to let her go. Caught between the two, he stood rooted to the spot, still holding her.

They stayed that way for a long time, and he knew that, whatever else happened, he'd remember this for as long as he lived.

Finally, she pulled away, but only slightly. She looked up into his eyes, ran a gentle hand through his hair.

"Come on," she whispered.

She took his hand and led him into the bedroom.

•

Later, much later, they lay together in his bed.

Morales had never felt more at peace in his life. He loved the way Tara nestled against him, her head resting on his chest.

She raised her head slightly and nuzzled against his cheek.

"I know," he said, "I need a shave."

"Uh-uh," she murmured. "I like it."

She ran a hand across his chest. Her fingers encountered the gold cross there. She picked it up and ran her thumb over it before looking at him.

"You're not gonna get all weird and guilty on me, are you? 'Cause I know what we did was prob'ly wrong. But for some reason I don't feel bad."

"Neither do I," he said. "I feel like this is where I should be."

She made a happy little sound and scrunched against him. He was bending down to kiss her when he heard the sharp knock on his door. He stopped, his lips scant inches from hers.

"*Damn* it," he heard her whisper, and for some reason, that struck them both as funny.

They began laughing, quietly at first, then they were trying to stifle the guffaws that threatened to erupt from them.

Tara kissed Morales on the neck.

"Maybe they'll go away," she whispered.

"I'll get rid of them," he said.

He got up and pulled on his jeans and T-shirt. He went to the front room and looked out the window.

A police car was sitting in the driveway.

Morales frowned. "What do they want now?"

He walked to the door and opened it. A man in a police uniform was standing there, but there was something off about him, something wrong. The cap was pulled down over his eyes, and the uniform hung loosely on him like the cast-off raiment of a scarecrow.

Then the man looked up. Morales saw who it was, and he felt his world begin to come apart.

"Howdy, Father," Clyde Stouffer drawled. He raised a black pistol and pointed it at Morales's face. "Did you enjoy fucking my wife?"

30

"FIRST THING I NEED YOU to tell me," Clyde said, "is where's the boy?"

Father Morales and Tara were seated at the dining room table, across from one another. Clyde paced back and forth, the gun in his hand pointing first at one of them, then the other, as if he couldn't decide which one to shoot first.

Tara was watching him, her eyes wide with horror.

"What boy?" Morales asked. "You mean the boy that was—" He stopped dead as the gun was suddenly in his face.

"You know goddamn well who I mean," Clyde growled. "Where the fuck is he?"

"Clyde," Tara said. "Baby, please..."

"Shut up, whore. I'ma deal with you later. Now where's that freaky little blind kid?"

"I don't know," Morales said. "He left with the people he showed up with. They're out of—"

The slash of the gun barrel across his face turned his words to a cry of pain and opened a gash across his temple.

Tara cried out.

Clyde turned the gun back to her. "I said SHUT THE

FUCK UP!"

"Clyde," she sobbed, "Please, baby, stop. You're sick. Something's got into your head."

Clyde ignored her. He turned the gun back to Morales. "Where's the boy?"

Morales was holding his hand against his head. He pulled it away and looked at it. It was covered with blood from the head wound. "I swear to you, I don't know."

"You left-handed or right-handed?" Clyde asked.

Morales looked at him uncomprehendingly. "What?"

"Left-handed," Clyde said, as if talking to a stupid child, "or right?"

A wicked looking knife appeared in his free hand. The gun never wavered from in front of Morales's face, and a feeling of dread stole over him as he realized what was about to happen.

"Clyde..."

"Choose, Father." Clyde almost spat the last word. "Or I swear to God, I'll start cutting on your girlfriend here. I'll shoot you, cripple you so you can't do anything, then I'll fuck her to death with this knife while you watch. You think I'm bullshitting, you just look up here in my eyes."

Morales didn't dare do that. He was too terrified of what he'd see there. Instead, he looked across the table. Tara had gone white with shock.

"I'm right-handed," he whispered.

"Then put your left hand on the table," Clyde said.

Tara's voice was a broken whimper. "Please. Don't."

Clyde ignored her. He stared at Morales, licking his lips. Slowly, Morales slid his left hand onto the table, fingers extended.

Tara let out a low moan of terror.

Clyde flipped the knife into a stabbing position in his left hand, still holding the gun on Morales with his right. He played the tip between Morales's splayed fingers.

"Now," he said, "where's the boy?"

Morales's voice was a choked whisper. "I don't know. I swear it."

Clyde raised the knife, then brought it down hard. It drove through the back of Morales's hand, splitting flesh, bone and tendon, the tip buried in the wood of the table.

Morales screamed, his howl of pain blending with Tara's cry.

Clyde left the knife where it was, studying Morales's face.

"Where is he?" he whispered. "*She* needs to know." He wiggled the handle slightly, causing Morales to whimper in agony.

"I don't know," Morales croaked. "I told you the truth. Please. How can I tell you what I don't know?"

Clyde seemed to think about that for a moment. Then he yanked the knife back out.

Morales yelped, then pulled his wounded hand back to wrap it under the other arm. He laid his head on the table, then raised it again, shamefully aware of the tears running down his face.

Clyde continued to regard him for a moment.

Morales's eyes were fixed on the knife in his hand. Then he noticed something. Through the haze of pain, he couldn't register at first what he was looking at. Then he saw the cuts on the young man's forearms, the dot-within-a-circle carved into the flesh.

He looked up into Clyde's eyes and saw the madness there. Only then did he know what he was dealing with. He racked his brain for what he could remember of the Rite he needed so desperately now.

"Put your other hand out, Father," the thing inside Clyde Stouffer crooned.

Father Esteban Morales looked Clyde in the eye as he put his hand on the table.

"I command you, unclean spirit," he said, struggling through a litany he barely remembered from seminary school, "whoever you are, along with all your minions now attacking this servant of God—"

He was interrupted by the descent of the knife into the back of his right hand, cleaving through the mortal flesh. The agony wrenched another scream from his throat.

"That's not gonna help you, priest. Now *where* is the boy?"

"He doesn't know, Clyde," Tara sobbed. "Stop. Please stop."

Clyde turned to her. "Your lover boy's not such a stud now, is he, *sweetheart*?"

He yanked the knife out again.

"I guess he's telling the truth, though. He's not brave

enough to lie after that."

He straightened up and pointed the gun at Tara.

"I guess *she*'s gonna have to be satisfied with the priest. But when she's done, you and I are gonna have a long, long talk. At least *I'll* be talking. You might find it a little hard once I cut out your lying tongue."

He motioned with the gun.

"Get moving."

31

"WESTON," THE GUARD SAID THROUGH the window of the holding cell. "You got a visitor."

Weston looked up. "Who?"

The guard, a slender black man who'd been reasonably courteous to him since his booking, shrugged his shoulders. "Says he's your lawyer."

Weston shook his head. "I didn't ask for a lawyer."

"Well, you got one. C'mon, get up. I got to take you to the visitin' room."

The visiting room of the county jail was a small, stark rectangle painted a sickly yellow color. The only furniture was an old wooden table bolted to the floor. Most of the paint had peeled off of it and off the pair of rickety wooden chairs bolted down on either side of it.

A man in a suit was seated at the table. He stood up as the guard brought Weston in.

"Ted Garcia," he said, extending his hand.

Weston looked him over as they shook hands. Garcia was a light-complected Latino with close cropped black hair. His linen suit looked expensive, as did the watch on his right wrist. He had large, expressive brown eyes behind a pair of dark-rimmed glasses.

"Thanks, Louis," he told the guard.

"I'm supposed to stay in the room," the guard said.

Garcia shook his head. "You know that's not how it works. This is my client. I'm his attorney."

The guard looked unhappy. "I know, Mr. Garcia. But Sergeant Paulson..."

Garcia shook his head in disgust. "Paulson. I should have known. Go ahead and leave us alone, Louis. I'll square things with the sergeant."

Louis still looked hesitant.

"Come on," Garcia said, "Paulson's order is bullshit, and you know it. I'm already going over his head on this one. I'll make sure you're covered."

"Well... okay," the guard said. He looked at Weston sternly. "You behave yourself now."

"He will," Garcia said. "I promise. Hey, how's that girl of yours, by the way?"

Louis grinned. "Got into Ole Miss."

Garcia made an exaggerated face of dismay. "Oh, I'm so *sorry*."

The guard laughed. "I know, you a 'Bama man."

"Roll, Tide," Garcia said. "Seriously, though. Congratulations."

"Thanks."

As the guard left, Garcia took a small black digital recorder out of a coat pocket and spoke into it. Weston wondered why he didn't just use his cell, but maybe phones weren't allowed in the visiting room.

"Pamela, let's send Louis Parker's girl Peggy some roses. 'Congratulations on getting into Ole Miss.' Thanks." He sat down across from Weston. "You'd be amazed at how far being nice to people can get you."

"Was that for my benefit?" Weston asked.

Garcia smiled. "Not really. Just making conversation." He looked at Weston for a moment. "So, Mr. Clean has you in custody for possession of a stolen firearm."

Weston was intrigued despite his suspicion. "Mr. Clean?"

"It's what they call Paulson around the courthouse. Not because he's incorruptible, although I've never heard anything that would suggest he's bent. It's because any time some old lady reports she's missing her jewelry, the first thing Paulson does is arrest the cleaning lady. Every damn time. Often on no evidence at all."

"You're saying he's a bad cop."

Garcia shook his head. "I'm saying he's a *terrible* cop. On the other hand, I'll miss him when he finally steps in it one too many times and gets canned. He always makes me look good."

"I'm happy for you," Weston said. "But why are you here?"

Garcia cocked his head to one side and observed him shrewdly. "You don't impress me as being naive enough to ask that question."

"I'm just saying, I didn't ask for a lawyer—especially one who's bound to cost me and arm and a leg—and you're too well dressed to be a public defender."

"Ah," Garcia said. "I see your point. Well, don't worry about it. Father Morales called me."

"That was nice of him. But didn't he take a vow of poverty? I doubt he can afford your parking fees, let alone your hourly rate."

Garcia nodded. "I know. But don't worry, I'm not charging him. I'm doing this in the hope that maybe at the next confession, he'll go a little easier on the Our Fathers and Hail Marys."

"Sounds like you have a lot of penance to do."

"Don't we all," Garcia said. "Anyway, I hear that Paulson's case against you two is about to fall apart. I talked with a nice young fellow named Griff who has some papers you asked for. He's bringing them to me, along with your car. It's ready, by the way. I understand these papers give you an alibi for the theft of the pistol in South Carolina."

Weston nodded. "Proof that we were in Missouri at the time it was stolen."

Garcia went on. "So what I've done is persuade the magistrate to hold off on actually charging you or setting bond until I can get those papers in hand, wave them under Paulson's nose, and threaten him with the Federal lawsuit he so richly deserves if he goes ahead with this nonsense. Sound like a plan?"

Weston thought for a moment, then nodded. "How long do you think it'll take?"

Garcia shrugged. "Not long, I hope. Close of business today."

Weston felt the Beast receding from them, getting farther and farther away. He wanted to grind his teeth in frustration.

Instead, he said, "Have you talked to Kate? How is she?"

"She's fine. Worried about you. And the boy... Christopher, is it?"

"Yeah. Can you help me get him out of wherever he is?"

"It's not my usual area of practice, but Becky Chance, the social worker who took him, is Child Protective Service's answer to Paulson. By which I mean she has more enthusiasm than sense. While I'm getting you two sprung, I think I can call the local Social Services director."

"And tell him what?"

"And persuade him that his department's limited budget and resources do not need to be spent on a child with some potentially expensive special needs, but who's in good health, at least minimally safe, and who, unless I miss my guess, will be out of sight, out of mind, and out of our great State of Alabama real soon now."

"Mr. Garcia," Weston said, "I can guarantee you that."

"Which raises the next question. Who is it that has such a grudge against you that they'd set your car on fire and try to frame you?"

Weston shrugged. "I don't know."

"You're lying," Garcia said without heat. "But whoever they are, you might want to stay away from them. They clearly don't like you very much."

"I will. I'll stay away from him."

Garcia sighed and got his feet. "You're lying again. But it's your life. *Vaya con dios*, Mr. Weston."

•

The campsite was upriver from where they'd entered the woods, in a well-hidden clearing surrounded by underbrush and cottonwood trees. There was a dead campfire in the center of the clearing, cold ashes and a single half-blackened log the only remnants.

Clyde had shackled Morales to a slender tree trunk, his back to the tree and his wounded hands secured behind him with a pair of police handcuffs.

Tara sat several feet away, her own hands bound behind her with duct tape. Clyde had secured her to another tree by a dog collar around her neck. The collar was attached to a length of chain that wrapped around a big cottonwood. She was sitting cross-legged, head bowed, like someone who'd given up hope and was waiting to die.

Morales wanted to try to comfort her, but Clyde had wrapped more duct tape around his head and mouth to keep him quiet.

Clyde was standing at the edge of the clearing, knife in one hand, gun in the other. His back was to them, his gaze fixed on the river.

Morales had lost track of how long he'd been like that, and how long they'd been here. He wondered what Clyde was waiting for, even as he dreaded the answer.

The words of a parishioner came back to him, spoken as he sat by the man's deathbed to offer words of comfort.

"I don't fear death, Father," the old man had said in a dry papery whisper. "But dying... it *hurts*."

Whatever death Clyde had planned for them, Morales knew, would be long and ugly and as painful as the thing inside him could make it. He'd run out of prayers, save one.

Lord, take me, he thought, but make him let Tara go. Don't make her suffer for my weakness.

He had no faith left that the prayer would be answered.

Gray clouds had been gathering overhead for the last hour, and Morales saw the quick flashbulb pulse of distant lightning against the darkening sky. A long while later, he heard the roll of faraway thunder.

Clyde turned at the sound and looked at them.

There was nothing human left in those eyes.

"It's almost time," he said. "Can you hear her?"

Morales shook his head. All he could hear was the rising wind and his own labored breathing. Then he began to detect something, at the edge of his hearing, like a conversation in another room he desperately needed to hear.

He strained to catch the sound, until he realized it was inside his head. And it wasn't conversation.

It was the sound of a woman singing.

32

IT WAS NEARLY SEVEN PM by the time they were finally released. A different guard from the one who'd first locked Kate up came to get her.

"We're being let go?" she asked. "Was the charge dismissed?"

"All I know is that we're to turn the two of you loose. I don't even think there was any charge. Least we didn't get any paperwork for one."

Kate shook her head in disbelief, wondering how the lawyer, Garcia, had managed to work such miracles. She'd been skeptical when he'd come to see her, but it sounded as if he'd done exactly what he promised.

She followed the jailer out to the processing area where she was given her clothing and belongings back. It felt good to be out of the loose fitting, scratchy jail jumpsuit.

Weston was waiting for her just outside the glass doors of the jail's front lobby.

"You okay?" he asked.

She nodded. "You?"

"Happy to be out of that cell, but that's about the extent of it. He got away from us. He was here the whole time, and he got away."

"I know," she said, and put a hand on Weston's shoulder. "But we'll get him. At least we've been heading in the right direction."

At that moment, a forest green BMW pulled up beside them. The driver's side window rolled down to reveal the smiling face of Ted Garcia. "Howdy folks. Got someone here who wants to see you."

The passenger door opened and Christopher got out.

"Chris!" Kate said, and ran to him. Weston followed. As Kate swept the boy up in a bear hug, Weston turned to Garcia.

"Thank you," he said simply.

"Glad to do it. Christopher's suitcase is in the trunk. And Noah, your car's in the visitor's lot, around the side. Father Morales paid the repair bill."

"I'm gonna go pay him back right now," Weston said.

"Say hey to him for me. Tell him I'll see him this Sunday."

"I will."

After they'd retrieved the case, Weston led them to the side lot. Kate sighed as she saw the battered Rambler. "Guess we're down to one car now."

•

They made the drive to Morales's house in exhausted silence. The clear skies had begun to cloud up, and the heavy air had the charged feel that preceded a summer thunderstorm.

When they arrived, they saw two cars in the driveway.

"Isn't that Tara's car?" Kate asked.

She and Weston looked at each other.

After a moment, Weston said, "Maybe we should knock first."

"Good idea."

Christopher spoke up from the back seat.

Something's wrong.

They both turned. "What? What's wrong?"

The boy's face was a mask of distress.

Something bad happened here. Something really bad.

"Stay in the car," Weston told him.

He got out and approached the house, slowly, like a man walking on an unknown street in an enemy town. Kate fell in beside him, wishing her gun wasn't still inside the house.

Weston turned slightly as if he was about to tell her to go back.

"Don't even start," she said.

He just shook his head and took the steps to the porch slowly, gingerly. From far away, Kate could hear a low rumble of thunder.

The door swung open at Weston's touch.

"Hello?" he called into the gloom of the house.

There was no answer. They entered and Weston snapped the lights on.

"Oh, my God," Kate said. "Noah. Look at the table."

The dining room table was covered in blood, the fluid beginning to congeal on the wooden top. As they drew closer, Kate could see that some of it had run off the edge and puddled on the floor.

He hurt him, Christopher said. *He hurt him bad.*

Kate and Weston turned to find Chris standing in the doorway, looking stricken.

"I told you to wait in the car," Weston said.

Kate walked over and knelt by the boy. "Who hurt who, Chris?"

Father Steve. Somebody hurt him. Hurt his hands. Then they took him. And Tara.

"Who hurt Father Steve, Chris? Was it Clyde?"

"Was it the Beast?" Weston asked.

Neither. Both. I can't tell. They're all... wrapped around one another. But they're all gone now. They left. He took them.

"Gone where?" Weston asked.

"Where do you think?" Kate said. "They went to the river."

She ran into the bedroom, got her Beretta and a pair of magazines. She shoved one into place and stuck the other one in the back pocket of her jeans. When she came out of the room, she saw Weston's eyes go to the weapon in her hand. He was holding his sketchbook and a pencil.

"Any objections?" she asked.

He shook his head.

"Good. Let's go. Unless you want to call the police again."

Weston grimaced. "I think we've seen enough of the local cops for one day."

•

Kate drove, with Christopher in the back seat. She could hear him, slowly rocking back and forth.

Weston was sketching frantically. She stole a look and sucked in a sharp breath.

He had drawn a pair of hands, like the famous "Praying Hands" picture seen in every Sunday School. But these hands had been horribly wounded, gashed open and covered in blood.

Somebody hurt his hands, Christopher had said.

As Weston tore that sheet away and started another drawing, Kate set her mouth grimly and sped up.

•

The singing had grown louder as the skies grew darker. It seemed to Morales to have no words, and the melody seemed never to resolve into something he could follow, but the song was irresistibly compelling.

"She's coming," Clyde said, and there was a strange awe and wonder in his voice.

He walked over to the tree where he'd bound Morales. He walked behind it, and a moment later, Morales's hands were free.

Morales brought them around in front of him, looked down, and groaned behind the duct tape. All he could feel in them was pain. He couldn't even close them to make a fist. There was no way to stop this madman with a gun from doing what he was about to do.

"Stand up," Clyde snarled at him. "Stand up, you Mexican son of a bitch."

Slowly, Morales got to his feet.

Clyde turned to Tara. "You too, whore. Get your ass up."

"Just kill me," she said in a small, hopeless voice. "I

know you don't love me no more, but just kill me. You ain't gotta torment me."

That seemed to stagger him for a moment. He stopped and looked down at Tara, breathing hard.

Morales saw his chance. He hated to leave her, but if he could get Clyde to focus his anger on him, chase him, maybe she'd have a chance to get free. Or he could find help. But he knew if he stayed here they'd both die.

He began to run, plunging out of the clearing and into the woods. He heard Clyde cursing behind him, then his heavy footfalls as the younger man gave chase.

Morales almost wept with gratitude. His biggest fear had been that Clyde, or whatever Clyde was by now, would simply threaten to torture Tara if he didn't come back.

But whatever was in him was a predator by nature.

We call him the Beast, Kate had said, and the nature of the Beast was to hunt.

Father Morales ran faster than he'd ever run in his life, pelting through the trees and undergrowth by the river, clawing with his useless fingers at the duct tape over his mouth. A blinding flash illuminated the night, followed by an ear-splitting crack of thunder. He heard Clyde cry out in surprise.

Come on, he thought. Follow me, Clyde. Come *on*.

It began to rain, huge wet drops pounding down out of the turbulent sky.

Then he heard the voice again.

It sounded as if it was coming from right beside him,

the song clearer to him now. It was achingly beautiful, and lonely. So lonely. It was breaking his heart.

She was breaking his heart.

He couldn't run away from it. He pulled up short, panting, all thought of the menace behind him gone from his mind. He felt a presence and turned, finally managing to pull the duct tape free of his mouth.

"Tara," he gasped.

But the figure in the trees wasn't Tara. He couldn't see her face, only a slender body, pale in the darkness. She had no clothing, but her long, thick red hair fell almost to her knees and wrapped around her, obscuring her nakedness.

"What...?" he said.

The slim figure held out a hand toward him.

Help me. Her voice was the voice of the singer he'd heard in his head. *I'm so cold. And so lonely. Help me. Please.*

He couldn't deny the summons. He took one staggering step toward the figure.

Then he began to run.

33

AS THEY PULLED UP TO the place where they'd first stopped the Rambler, lightning split the sky and the thunder detonated like an atomic bomb, seemingly right above them.

Kate and Weston both flinched. The rain began to pour down, the wind blowing great sheets of water across their vision.

"Wonderful," Kate said. "How are we gonna find them in all this?"

"Follow me," Weston said grimly. "Christopher just showed me."

"He showed you where they are?"

Weston shook his head. "He showed me where *she* is. And that's where Clyde is taking them."

"*She*? She who?"

"You've met her before. She's the thing that lives in the river. And she's hungry."

Her name was Chloe, Christopher said. *But no one's called her that in a long time. Not since the man killed her.*

"What man?" Kate asked. She was still trying to wrap her head around what was going on.

The man she thought loved her. The man who was

the father of her baby. And she's not just hungry. She's angry.

"Come on," Weston said as he opened the car door. "We need to stop her."

"From doing what?"

He turned. "I've only got bits and pieces from what Chris showed me, but I think the Beast made some kind of deal with this thing. She kept him hidden. In return, he offered her sacrifices." He looked in the back seat. "He offered her a child."

Kate's hand went to her mouth. "You mean *Christopher?*"

"Yeah," Weston said. "She almost took him earlier, remember? She was drawn to him. And he to her. I think she's attracted by his power. So I think the Beast offered to help her take him. Only he left before he could do it."

"But now Chris is here," Kate said. "And *we* brought him."

Weston nodded and looked into the back seat. "Chris, this time you need to stay in the car. And I mean it. Don't come down there."

I can help, the boy said.

"No!" Weston barked. "She almost took you once. She'll try again."

I know her now. I can talk to her.

"I said *no*, son, and I meant it. Now *stay here.*"

With that, he pulled himself up and out of the car.

Kate followed.

•

That strange tuneless song seemed to be throbbing like a migraine in Morales's head, drowning out all thoughts but one.

She needs help. She needs me.

In his mind, the dimly seen figure in front of him began to look like Tara. So slender, and so frail looking...

Yes, the figure sang. *Come to me. Help me. Be with me.*

He drew closer.

The woman was standing on the edge of the river. He could see that the water was up, fed by the storm. Eddies swirled around her bare feet. She had her head down so he couldn't see her face. That long red hair that hid her nakedness seemed to move of its own volition, squirming about her body like a nest of snakes.

But that can't be right, he thought. Tara has blonde hair...

He drew up short, a scant foot away from her.

"I'm here, love," he panted. "I can help you."

I know, she said.

The long red hair reached out for him, wrapped around him, then pulled him toward her, into her outstretched arms.

She looked up and he saw her face for the first time.

And Esteban Morales screamed.

•

The minute Kate exited the car, she was drenched. The water poured down out of a sky that seemed alive with light and rolling thunder.

Weston was a barely visible shadow moving away from her in the dark until a flash of lightning illuminated him like a man on a stage.

Kate swore under her breath and racked the slide on her pistol to chamber a round. She didn't know how much use a gun would be against whatever the hell was in that river, but she didn't know what else to do. Besides, if Weston was right, Clyde was still down here, and dangerous.

A terrible scream echoed through the night, a man's anguished howl of terror.

"Morales!" she heard Weston call back.

There was a bright flash off to her right that wasn't lightning, and she heard the sharp report of a gunshot, followed by a curse from Weston.

She could briefly make out a shape in the darkness behind the muzzle flash. Her reflexes took over and she dropped into firing position, knees slightly bent.

"POLICE!" she called out. "DROP THE WEAPON!"

The only answer was another shot, this one aimed at her. She could hear the whine of the bullet, passing only inches from her left ear.

She still couldn't make out who was firing, but the next flash of lightning gave her a brief glimpse of two figures standing about twenty yards away.

Tara was in front, her mouth open, her eyes wide with fear. Kate couldn't see who was behind her, but his arm was wrapped around the girl's body, pulling them tightly together, and she knew it had to be Clyde.

The other arm was extended toward Kate, the gun pointed straight at her.

As the afterimage of the lightning faded, the blast of the gun was drowned out in the crack of thunder overhead.

Kate dropped to the ground.

•

Weston made his way through the tall grass near the river, close to where they'd found Clyde passed out before.

As he approached, he could see Morales through the trees, standing next to the water. There was a shadow looming over him, one Weston had seen before. It seemed to wrap itself around the priest's body, obscuring him from sight.

Then Morales screamed.

"MORALES!" Weston called out.

Before he could say another word, he heard the sound of a gunshot and felt something burning in his right leg. He swore as his leg gave way, pitching him forward into the tall grass.

When he looked down, he saw blood staining the fabric of his jeans. He heard another gunshot and looked up. Kate was shouting something, but he couldn't make out the words.

He looked down at his leg again. The next flash of lightning showed a long tear in the fabric.

Just grazed me, he thought with relief.

He heard the sound of another gunshot, followed by a woman's cry.

Kate, he thought. Clyde's shooting at Kate.

He rolled over and began to rise to his feet. As he put a hand down to steady himself, he felt something hard protruding from the ground beneath his fingers.

He looked down and saw a large rock, half buried in the ground. He gritted his teeth, closed his fingers tighter around the exposed portion of the rock, and pulled. The stone came free with a wet sucking sound.

Weston stood, hefting the rock in his right hand. He looked back at the river. He could hear the sounds of a struggle, but he couldn't see Father Morales.

"Sorry, Father," he muttered under his breath.

He began moving through the tall grass, crouched down, toward the place where he'd heard the shots. He strained his ears, trying to hear something over the roar of the rain. The water was running down his forehead and into his eyes.

As he wiped it away with his free hand, a dark shape rose out of the grass.

Clyde Stouffer stood there grinning, holding Tara in front of him to shield himself as he pointed the gun directly into Weston's face. He had his sleeves rolled up and Weston saw the bloody outline of the dot within a circle carved into his forearm.

"Boo," Clyde said.

34

WESTON DROPPED THE ROCK. "Don't do this, Clyde."

"Don't do what? Don't kill you? Weren't you about to bash my head in with that fuckin' rock?"

Weston had to raise his voice to be heard above the wind and the rain.

"You've got something riding you, son. Something evil. But I know there's gotta be enough of Clyde Stouffer left in there to throw it off." He gestured at Tara. "Something's left of the man who won this girl's heart. Be that man again, Clyde. Be him again."

For a moment, Clyde's eyes seemed to lose the glint of madness. The gun in his hand wavered slightly.

Tara spoke for the first time. "Please baby. Don't—"

There was another cry from the trees by the river. It was Morales's voice.

Tara stopped mid-sentence and her head jerked toward the sound.

Clyde's face darkened. "You want to go to him, bitch? Then go." He shoved her away, so hard that she stumbled. As she fought to regain her balance, Clyde raised the gun and shot her in the back.

As Tara pitched forward, Weston heard Kate scream. "Clyde, NO!"

Clyde fired again, then Weston heard the report of Kate's pistol. The shot went wide with no effect.

Clyde turned and fired in her direction. Weston heard Kate shout something, then Clyde turned to Tara, lying full length on the ground, and fired again.

Her body jerked as the round hit home.

Weston moved toward him, but the gun swung in his direction, stopping him dead in his tracks. Clyde looked at Tara, grinning madly, and raised the gun to put a third shot into her back.

From the tree line something *screamed.*

Weston turned in time to see it hurtling at them, bursting out of the trees by the river. It was made of shadows darker than the night that surrounded them, and it rolled across the ground like an oncoming dust storm.

Clyde cried out in fear and tried to aim the gun, but the thing was upon him before he could pull the trigger.

Weston saw the shadows become more substantial, black oily tentacles wrapping around the terrified man in front of him. They made a sound like whips striking flesh. With each impact, Clyde shrieked. It was a horrible sound of agony, worse even than Morales's cries of fear and despair.

It sounded as if Clyde was being skinned alive.

Almost worse than his animal howls was the screaming Weston could hear in his head, the raw sound of rage that came from the thing that enveloped Clyde. Whatever was inside him was howling back, the two voices sounding like wild animals rending one another in a fight to the death.

The water spirit—the *rusalka*—began to move toward the river, dragging Clyde with it, still wrapped in those horrible ropes of darkness. A flash of lightning illuminated the scene, and for a second, Weston saw through the cloud, saw the pale creature inside moving so fast it seemed to have a dozen arms and legs, all of them flailing at the man it held helplessly, each blow tearing another hysterical wail from his tortured body and soul.

Kate walked up next to him, the gun at her side, her eyes wide with shock.

"STOP!"

The shout came from the same area from where the shadow had come. Weston tore his horrified gaze away from what was happening to Clyde and turned to look.

Father Esteban Morales staggered out of the trees, weaving from side to side like a drunken man. The shadow-thing stopped moving, and Clyde's screams died to low whimpers, like a whipped dog.

The rain was slackening, the thunder now coming from farther away. As Morales approached, he raised something in his right hand. It was the cross from around his neck.

He came closer and began to speak in a hoarse, half strangled voice.

"*Requiem aeternam dona eis, Domine,*" he croaked, "*et lux perpetua luceat eis.*"

The *rusalka* seemed to recoil slightly, but it stayed

where it was.

Morales spoke again, stronger this time. "*Requiem aeternam dona eis, Domine, et lux perpetua luceat eis.*"

As Weston watched in amazement, the shadow began to dissipate. The darkness began to thin, just as the clouds above them were beginning to break up.

"*Requiem aeternam dona eis, Domine, et lux perpetua luceat eis,*" the priest said again, his voice rising to a shout.

"What's he saying?" Weston asked Kate. "Some kind of exorcism?"

"'Grant to them eternal rest, Lord,'" Kate whispered, "'And may light eternal shine upon them'. It's the beginning of the Mass for the Dead."

She doesn't need an exorcism, Christopher said. *She needs rest.*

Weston turned. Christopher was walking up to stand between him and Kate.

Weston frowned. "I told you to—"

"Hush," Kate said, and took Christopher's hand.

After a moment, Weston took his other one. He looked back to where the shadow-thing had been.

Clyde lay stretched out on the ground moaning.

Beside him stood a young woman, dressed in an antique-looking homespun frock. Her thick red hair was woven into a braid that extended to the middle of her back.

Weston recognized the girl from the picture Christopher had showed him, but instead of rage and malice, her face held a sense of wonder, as if she was seeing something never seen in her world before.

She held out her hand to the priest. He tried to take it, but his own hand went through it like fog.

Morales smiled and made the sign of the cross instead.

"Go in peace, Chloe, child of God. We'll be back. We'll find you. We'll find your bones. I promise. On my word. We'll give you rest."

The girl nodded, then smiled back. It was a beautiful smile.

Then she was gone.

Morales let out a long, shuddering breath. He stumbled over to where Tara lay on the ground face down. He knelt beside her body.

"No," he whispered. "No. Please, God. No. Take me and not her. Please."

There was no answer.

35

"IN PARADISUM DEDUCANT ANGEL," ESTEBAN Morales said.

May the angels lead you into paradise.

To a casual observer, it would have seemed a strange sight. A tall man, dressed in priest's white robes and stole, his hands heavily bandaged, standing in a wood by a river and apparently addressing the roots of a large tree.

Three people stood a few feet behind him, heads bowed: a woman in jeans and a white blouse, a man in slacks and a faded polo shirt, and a young boy with milky white eyes.

The man in the polo shirt was holding a shovel in one hand, a simple wooden cross in the other.

"In tuo adventu suscipiant te martyrus, et perducant te in civitatem sanctam Jerusalem, the priest went on.

At your coming may the martyrs receive you and lead you to the holy city of Jerusalem.

"Chorus angelorum te suscipat et cum Lazaro, quondam paupere, aeternam habeas requiem."

May the chorus of angels receive you and with Lazarus, once poor, may you have eternal rest.

"Amen," the priest concluded.

"Amen," the man and the woman repeated.

The boy was silent.

The man with the shovel and cross stepped forward. He leaned the cross against the tree and used the shovel to excavate a small hole.

When he was done, he took the cross and placed it upright into the hole before filling it again. For good measure, he pounded it down a little deeper with the flat of the shovel.

He stepped back and surveyed his handiwork.

Written on the flat surface facing them were the words CHLOE BAUER 1880-1897.

Esteban Morales took a long look at the impromptu grave marker and began unwrapping the stole from around his neck, his bandaged hands clumsy.

"So that's my last service," he sighed. "I probably should have gotten another priest to do this. A real one. But I really have no idea how I'd explain what needed to be done."

"I think she would have wanted you to do it," Kate Messenger said. "You promised her, after all." She put a hand on his arm. "You didn't let her down."

The priest looked at the boy, still standing quietly a few feet away.

"You're sure this is where the man buried her," he said. "The man who murdered her."

Christopher nodded.

She said to thank you. She's at peace now.

Morales stared at him, then shook his head.

Noah Weston spoke up. "We need to get on the road,"

he said, and held out his hand to Morales. "Thanks for opening your home to us, Father. Sorry about all the trouble."

Morales took the offered hand and shook it. "I think you can start calling me Esteban. Even though the official orders haven't come down, I'm done with the priesthood."

Weston shook his head. "You gave that girl's soul peace. Sounds like the work of a priest to me. A real one, no matter what some paper from a bureaucrat in a robe has to say."

"Let me guess," Morales said with a smile. "You're a Southern Baptist."

"Born and raised. A little backslid, though."

"Aren't we all," Morales said, then looked at his watch. "I've got to get going, too. I'm supposed to meet with the assistant D.A. who's prosecuting Clyde Stouffer. Not sure what I'm going to say to him, either. 'Well, Mister DA, I believe Clyde murdered a police officer and tried to kill his wife because he was the victim of... well, I'm not completely sure what.'"

He spread his hands helplessly.

"He didn't kill the officer," Weston said as the four of them began walking back to their cars. "You know that."

"Well, you say *you* know that. And I believe you. But again, how in the world do I explain the source of my knowledge about a mysterious traveling serial killer who cuts out people's tongues? I tell them everything you've told me, and they'll lock me in the padded cell next to Clyde's. And I can't let that happen."

"No," Kate told him, "you can't. Tara's got a long road ahead of her to recovery. Not just the bullet wounds. And she's gonna need you."

"I know."

They had reached the hard road where his Camry was parked behind Weston's Rambler.

"Well," he said, "I guess this is goodbye."

Weston opened the driver's side door. "You take care, Father."

Morales didn't bother to correct him. "You, too."

He turned to Kate. To his surprise, she gave him a quick, fierce hug.

When she pulled away, she was smiling. "Go with God, Esteban."

"And you, Kate."

As she got into the car, he turned to Christopher, who was just opening his door.

"Christopher," he said.

The boy stopped and turned, his sightless eyes toward Morales.

"What are you, child? Are you an angel? A demon? Or something else?"

Again, there was no answer. The boy just smiled and got into the car.

Morales watched them for a long time as they drove away.

EPILOGUE

"The difficulty is not so great to die for a friend, as to find a friend worth dying for."

~Homer

36

THEY'D BEEN ON THE ROAD for hours, passing from Alabama down toward the Florida Panhandle. They couldn't be sure they were even going in the right direction, but news of a series of murders in Tallahassee had come over the radio and Christopher had insisted they head that way.

Kate was taking her turn at the wheel, trying to accustom herself to the unfamiliar vehicle.

Weston had watched her closely the first hundred miles or so, clearly unsettled at the prospect of someone else driving his precious car, but after a while, he'd relaxed and even dozed in the passenger seat.

They were a few miles past the border when Christopher suddenly cried out.

"What?" said Weston, startling awake.

He turned back to look.

"What?" he said again when he saw the stricken expression on Christopher's face.

In answer, the boy cried out again, a heartrending sound of loss. Kate pulled the car to the side of the road. She put the vehicle in Park and looked back as well.

"What's wrong, Chris?"

Tears were streaming down his face as he spoke in their minds.

She's gone, he said. *Lucy. I can't hear her.*

Weston and Kate looked at one another.

"What do you mean?" Kate said. "Is she..." she stopped, unwilling to even suggest what she feared.

I don't know.

They could feel his panic.

"Is something drowning her out?" Weston asked. "Like in Singer?"

No. This is different. She's just... gone.

"Okay," Weston said. "It's okay. We'll find her."

"How?" Kate asked.

"We do what we do. We follow the trail of the Beast. We find him, we find her. And if we find him and she's not... with him..." Weston's face was grim. "We make him pay."

Kate looked at him for a long moment. Then, without speaking, she put the car in gear and got back on the road.

We hope you enjoyed this book, and if you did, we'd greatly appreciate a quick review on Amazon, Goodreads and other review sites. And be sure to tell your friends about the book as well. Reader recommendations go a long way toward spreading the word about a good book.

If you have any questions about the Linger Series or any of our other books, feel free to contact us at *BraunHaus-Media.com*.

Thank you.

Robert Gregory-Browne
Editorial Director
Braun Haus Media, LLC

www.ingramcontent.com/pod-product-compliance
Lightning Source LLC
Chambersburg PA
CBHW031947170626
46807CB00006B/2384